Diary
of a
DEAD MAN

By

SETH ALLEN MATHEWS

To A Love That Never Dies:
writing, poetry, literature,
family and friends
who have stood by my side.

And,
a special thanks to my father for telling me
"You can do whatever you put your mind to"
and my brother for telling me
"Make a book out of that short story."
I owe my father, mother, and brother the most.
A debt I may never repay.
Thank you.

Prologue

Drunk, drank too much, swished the dark liquid back, ambrosia for the wicked, another night I sinned, over-indulge to excess, pickled my brain, rendered me beyond, gone, gone again, a grievous delirium. Shapes cover the ceiling. Plaster above lined with some shapes, some blue, others spin, brown, triangles. I see shapes in my sickness. What sort of skulduggery is this? Pity me. I do. Ashamed yet again for hearts content, acid and blood creeping up the back of my throat, bile, vile existence. I cough and cough, weak at the arms as I roll to one side, the throbbing of a jackhammer bludgeoning my brain. My skin dry from intoxication, lack of water leaves me ill, dehydrated, perspiration needles at my glands, pits of a nickel-dime shirt stained from sweet sweat of medium-shelf liquor. The smell, rich as gasoline, tempted to inhale, yet daring for not too long. I should get up, shower, work on my manuscript, get out of this manic state as my mind races, the past was harsh like inhaling cigar smoke, my lungs weak for the cause. Where do I go from here, oh how I know my past, people near have muff-covered ears for the winter of my tale, only opening for warmth, as for the cold of my existence, the frost, nobody cares to endure the story of a weak old man, a man bitter with age.

Cracked and frayed, my mattress is threadbare, shaped in place where a body rested for a spell. Edged with yellow stains of mildew and nights where heads propped to not choke on puke like the King. Real drunks

1

don't choke on their puke and die, I am a real drunk. Dying, dying is a hell of a way, a path, journey we all take, the end is always near, but never in sight until one's time comes. We know of an end, when is the question we refrain to inquire for the answer, I know my time is near, near the brink, where do I cross over to? Tales of old speak of places, places where one may find solace, I believe that would be nice, nice to find peace for once. My heart pounds, beats that are timed on a clock running out of batteries, juice, I knew the alcohol, drugs, cigarettes, wild evenings and into early mornings would wear out my power source quickly, faster than I expected, the time was near.

Empty as a house can get with my wife deceased, children gone, dog dead and buried in the back forty by a willow tree that sways with the wind, a willow that weeps as much as my insides, as much as the thought of an empty bed where I am the one to come home alone to, to heat, sprawl which I do not, as if she would rise from the ashes like a great phoenix to bring warmth to my restless nights again where my sorrows plague my sanity. Years have passed, long has it been since visitors came to knock at my door and bellow my name, to snap me out of a drunken stupor in my studies, save one friend that still comes by on occasion, he is not a visitor though, family never visits.

They always stay with you, in your blood.

To face the window where an old oak scratches the glass like nails on a chalkboard. Mrs. Nutimaker used to wake me from my slumber that way years ago. Decades have passed since class, since junior high when those better days transpired and were as palpable as the bottle resting two feet from the throw of my bed on a cottonwood chest weighted with clothes and trinkets. I gander out the window where foliage clouds most of my view, where sun beams in to blind my eyes, the day will come and go like it invariably does. The chance I take to turn my back and see an empty spot next to me, where she used to lie, my wife, who had gone and left long before her time was truly through, long before the kids graduat-ed, or long before I became a grandfather to three and she a grandmother.

Void, abyss, darkness in the valley, so much light comes through dou-ble-paned glass in my home older than I, bright on the surface as it burns white weathered skin, cracked by many years, but never penetrating to the depths within. Heat attempted to force the toxins out, a futile shot, as if it were to cleanse my system of cancer, I would ask why, why did my Maybelline, why did she deserve to perish while I still walk this earth. Nature tries to save, prosper, but I am a long case short of time. Miracles only happen on the black and white shows that flicker as a cheap antenna loses signal, my reception to this life is the same: faint and dwindling.

What kind of life is left for a man who knows the pitch black of an afterlife waits around every corner, close enough to grab, tantalizing weak arteries with fright. The hollow section of me would wish to say I do not fear what is to come, that what shall consume will only be what it is, what it always is, the end. Braver men than I have claimed, lied to the faces of those who listen, I speak truth, sincerity, interest it may not for whom enjoy an epic tale preached from noble's bard. For I fear death as it will come, hallucinations of a hooded man, the one to take my soul. Where will my ego go, what will this future of mine entail, is there a future yet after death? Answers I search for but never find, dark ambrosia slurped in haste as I look, through book after book, text unrevealing, context unsure.

Inside I bleed, wish it were shallow, the chasm gaping and grand, whittled by bone, in essence from truly being alone. A disease that reaps, destabilizes the structure, debilitated as they come, I lay here dying. Death, I knew it to be cold, colder than cold: subzero. My children are distant when I am here with no comfort but the end, a bottle of whisker-growing whiskey, and a long windy story to finish.

1

A time long ago, I was a decent man, good as they come, modest and wise with a smile creasing my face, lips licked to fight back peeling skin, stubble in sight, a hat propped over standard hair, crew cut for a man, dirty blonde and strait as an arrow. Eyes as blue as glaciers, slow with movement, piqued by curiosity a time or two before. Clothes were a statement, I shined like a diamond in the rough, a rugged man, but gentle as drifting sand. Adorned by a tie and hat, polished black leather shoes, laces knotted twice, slicked back mane, toothpick nestled between clenched teeth. I have been old-fashioned before common crowds scantily clad in decorated T's, baggy pants, and cellphones were a commodity. Style was a particular attribute many lacked, class came few, far, seldom between.

The days were fast like moving clouds, deceptive, by the time I knew it nineteen summers had passed since my mother released me from her womb. School was a thing of the past, big ticket items, money, and a desperation for companionship were all my jubilant eyes could see. Class never held appeal after I learned to teach, under my own tutelage I ascended far above any expectation of my peers. Why bother with college when an aptitude for progress was fed best by hardbacks and experience in the real world. Ironic, I knew how to teach with sophistication, I thought about giving back, but never came a time where leading a room full of adolescents in a subject came to be.

Monday through Friday, fifty hours a blistering week were spent hammering railroad spikes into rigid ground. A crew of ten started at the station on Main Street, Carlton, Oregon, where we broke our backs for bread money. A task such as this to link my hometown to the tracks on the outskirts of Yamhill coming from the small town of Gaston and leading to a more populated city, made a man out of the boy I was. Toiling, we thrust our trusty spike mauls, akin to the sledgehammer of today, thirty-six inches long and twelve pounds, the majority of the weight rested in an elongated steel head. When work started, I had chicken arms compared to what they became. Twelve hours a day for a week at a time made a boy stocky and not a weakling anymore. A strong character was developed as well, a higher percentile of my crew was white, two black men worked alongside me. In the past and present I had never been a racist, judging a man by the color of his skin was to judge a book by its cover before reading the contents. I was neither a fool nor ignorant, I gave everyone a chance.

Derogatory terms were yelled, "John Henry would be abashed at you two coons! Slower than molasses in January." Distant words reverberating through the two black mens' spines, I could see it chilled their bones as I read behind their eyes. We worked neck and neck with one another, the other men stayed clear, uncalled for names were spoken, not close, no, Abe and Josiah would end a man as easily as a fly with sheer mass. Coffee-black skin, brothers I was told, they were defined, physiques of statues sculpted by an artist. Their attitudes were better than mine, reserved, when an insult darted their way they only shrugged it off, as I should have.

"Keep to yourself, Larson! No one was bothering you!" Words left my mouth without realizing what price would come. Abe looked at me and shook his head, a smile parted his lips, Josiah knew what was coming as well.

"Hank, you stickin' up for them colored folk." Six men came behind Larson, none as sizable as Abe nor Josiah, but all made me look like a toothpick. I was good, exceptional at learning when it came to books.

As far as keeping my mouth shut, I was unable to pick that up when I knew better.

Throaty as a voice came, Abe said over to me, "Drop your gloves, we will show them callused hands as they flash like lightning to their eyes." Adrenaline squeezed my lungs, I took my gloves off, my heart sped, thumping, pressing at my rib cage, it hurt though it felt right. "You too, Jo." Josiah nodded, he was quiet from what I gathered.

"Shut that yap of yours, cur. You stand for these dogs, you're no better than 'em." Hate- laced words stabbed and injected like epinephrine. Larson was a daft man, some never get that we are equal, we all have the same rights as individuals. Man, woman, all are subjected to earth where we share commonality, no one is superior, it is only a troubled ego that thinks that way, like Larson's.

"Tick tock, tick tock", I tapped my wrist impatiently, tired of wasting time listening to hogwash. "Did you walk all the way down here to assert your stupidity? Walk away and work in peace, we mean no harm." Trying to be a mediator and actually being one are distinctly contrasting.

"Respect your common man, Hank, not them, them aren't worth the air we breathe, why we allow them that much I don't know." Men nodded in unison from Larson's band. The three of us stood stock-still like frozen lily pads on a pond in December, holding the inferno at bay, blood started to boil, tension was in the air. It was about to go down, I'd give each racist a lick if they came my way.

Josiah could wake the dead with a voice such as his, "Hank said, walk," enunciating each word, "I suggest that you do." Concise and to the point, no room for deliberation, it was our turn to nod our heads. My arms were crossed and hands fixed in either armpit, until I "instigated", as my foreman would tell me at a later date. Clapping my dominant right hand, licking my lips as I mouthed the words "bye, bye bye" to beckon Larson on his way. If our adversaries were intimidated, it was not from me, having strong black giants to your right and left startled an average man.

Serendipitous it was, spike mauls were left behind as seven strong came, Abe whistled his annoyance through a gap in his front teeth. I only chuffed like a happy dog. Our mauls were also left behind as fists clashed, elbows, even a knee to a man's groin via my quick-witted response to a lick at the jaw that rattled my brain. Josiah smashed his fists like hammers, knocking two men into the ground like spikes, Abe swatted one back to my mirth.

With pride, I challenged Larson to a duel, his fists moved double-quick, snapping at the wind, making a sound like a shot rubber band. Blood blotched my lip, neck and wool work shirt, as Larson's first, second, and third fist connected, to my dismay. The pleasure was all mine as I spat into a racist's eye, Larson cursed, apparently it burned, following up with a headbutt, his nose would never be ruler straight again, aquiline now like an eagle's beak. I choked on raspy breaths of air, air I shared with the black men, equitable, fair, who was to say different.

Hands on knees, I rested, Abe and Josiah patted my back, men ran back to work as they should, while others groveled on packed chestnut-colored soil. With a smoker's laugh, I snickered, as did my new friends. Pick your battles wisely and don't shy away from what is right. Actions, small or big, by and large, will impact your life, I understood that.

No one had asked me to put my neck out for those two. The fact that I did, established a rapport between the three of us. We put our gloves on and went back to work as Larson walked away, handkerchief spotted with red splayed across his face, slurring as normal, some things you can't alter. Who was the dog now, he and his affiliated six walked with their tails tucked between their legs. Shunned by three.

2

There had been a pub back then down the street from the station, three blocks distance where the proprietor allowed Abe, Josiah and I to be patrons, provided we did not cause a ruckus of course. A drinking problem is hard to kick like cancer, acquiring an intemperance at the age of nineteen that stuck with me ever since.

Sitting at the bar on a lacquered maple swivel stool worn by years of friction from trousers and occasionally a woman daring enough to wear a skirt. The latter came to mind as I dropped my jaw at a lassie three seats down sipping a mint julep like she was at the racetrack. Her skirt was acceptable, not too high up as to reveal more than a man's eye should see and not too low as to drape over knees. She had a pinup girl's figure, a woman all the way around, adorned with a button nose, matching black and white attire, and elegant shoulder length raven black hair with a slight crimp at the tips. Deep in concentration, brow furrowed, chin rested on the palm of a hand as legs were crossed, eyes darting, tracing an anal-retentive paper free of any ruffles.

A bartender approached me to ask as I was caught gawking at the fine young lady, "What'll you 'ave lad?" His mustache twined and curled once over, gray with age, a crooked smile, and crinkled skin from decades of smoking like a chimney.

"Round up an old-fashion for me, sir," I replied, looking over to Abe and Josiah, showing them a bill rubbing between index and thumb as to imply their first drink was on me.

A plume of smoke emitted from our bartender as he queried Abe, "You drinking, boy?"

"Take a Manhattan, sir." I smirked, his drink was named after a city far more vast than here.

"And you, son?" Josiah looked up to the stars as he kneaded his brain to decide what he would imbibe.

Clapping like thunderclouds, he told him, "Give me your special you got marked on the board." He raised a hand large as a spatula, meaty fingers the length of unsharpened pencils, pointing at a sign no bigger than a cafeteria's tray.

"There's two marked, will you take our gin Rickey, or the seven and seven, son?"

"Do the seven."

Drinks came around, we had three or four apiece by the time my lips were numb and desperate for a kiss, I looked over to see Lady Luck down there by herself, content with an article in the front page of the newspaper. A veritable bombshell. The boys looked at me, Abe punched my arm, "Get her, Hank." Gulping syrupy saliva down, I rose, straightened my blazer and cap, slacked my tie to give me room to breathe. Thankfully, I had changed into something nice before we rocketed down to the local drinking hole.

"Make sure you two train your eyes on your own business until I get back, don't need either one of you scaring her off." They both looked at me as if I were stupid.

In unison they mentioned, "Us, you're the one going to scare her off with that five dollar tie and seven dollar watch."

"Graduation present", I couldn't afford either, "be back in a bit."

Smoke was heavy in the air, everyone chain-smoked back before we knew it resulted in cancer. Sashaying down a few steps, as if to grab her attention, she never looked, intent on the newspaper. Nerves kicked in, so I tossed a filtered cigarette in my mouth, brought out a box of matches from my inner pocket, struck, inhaled and exhaled. Soothed by the motion, I asked the lassie, "May I sit?" She looked up at me, smiled, began to preen her hair, my cheeks turned red as a lobster.

"You are more than welcome," her voice smoother than honey.

Extending my hand to introduce myself, I said, "Name's Hank, Hank Shine."

"Maybelline Wick, but you can call me May if you like," she said in turn, took the silk dove-white glove off her hand, shook, and from that first interaction I was head over heels.

May was two years older than I, and lived in town where her apartment overlooked the park a street over from the bar. With nostalgia, I told her of my parents' place down Kutch Street at the end not far from here, she giggled saying, "Nothing is far in a wee quaint town like this." Maybelline was right, she bore with me as I disclosed my upbringing down Kutch in an A-frame house, I spent my juvenile years encouraged to attend school, partake in sports, fish down at the lake and in the river where the water rippled slow with its current. She took the time too, evidently she was born and raised in Salem, Oregon in a town quite like this: Aumsville. "A peaceful do-good place" she informed me. Recently moving into town as a convenience, she worked at the bank, a two-minute walk from here.

"As a matter-of-fact," she said, "I was rather poor, working the tracks did not pay a tinker's damn, enough to keep me afloat. But nothing to run home and tell mother about. Banks were for people with money, besides after the Great Depression, I was hardly willing to be invested. Wise choice. I reckoned. Not placing all my eggs in one basket, Dad learned the hard way when the stock market crashed and we were barely capable of keeping a roof over our heads."

May may work with money, though whether I had any or not did not seem to concern her, easy to figure out how destitute I was after I mentioned what my job was at the time. I carried myself well, frankly that showed more than money ever would.

"You or the lady need a refill?" The barkeep asked with prudence, noticing our glasses were empty.

I was tipsy, trying to stare at our server right in the eye with aplomb,

I said, "Yes, sir, take another round." Rapping my knuckles twice on the varnished walnut bar.

"Same cocktail?", he asked.

"Yes, sir, May would you care for another?" Her eyes locked mine, she batted soft eyelashes.

"Sounds marvelous,"

I liked the way she spoke. Her presence left a good impression, a woman should learn from her, I noted in my drunken haze, grinning from cheek to cheek.

"Okay, be back right quick." And he was, the light reflecting off his stainless steel cocktail shaker, he was smoking a cigarette down to the filter, singeing the hair of his mustache that crept below his top lip.

Suave in mannerism, I tipped him a dollar to look like a hotshot, stubbed my cigarette butt in a porcelain ashtray, took a nip from my glass and directed my attention back to May. "You care to play a game of pool?"

"If you are up for a challenge." A girl with confidence, I adored that. Her dimples showed and left an impression in my mind to this day.

Grabbing our glasses, I led her over to the pool table across the room from Abe and Josiah. There was a platform near where I deposited our drinks, fishing a nickel out of my pocket for the game, inserted it in the mechanism to the side, and the billiard balls dropped. The felt was a scarlet and the balls were shiny as my father's bald spot in the sun. Diamonds that marked the perimeter of the table were honed from an elephant tusk prior to ivory laws that banned the use of such a beautiful material. After racking for a standard game of 8-ball, May told me to hold on a moment before I broke. She made her way over to a jukebox next to an older couple sitting in a booth, I grinned as the music commenced.

"You like jazz, don't you?" asking me as if it were amoral, taboo to think otherwise, jazz was in everything, jazz was life.

"Course, would be outlandish not to." I chalked my tip, bowed my cue stick as I connected with the cue ball, slingshotting it down the length of the table, with success I made two solids on a break.

"Adept?" Her response to an eased start to our game, I was trying, at minimum, to be her equal. I hate losing, but I'd throw a game to win a girl over every time.

"Grew up playing with my older brother Chad." My only brother, not that it would have made a difference if I had two, he died before he could relish my valedictorian speech. Not a day goes by that he isn't missed. A drastic car accident cost him his life. Seatbelts were not enforced and airbags were few and far between, implemented years hence. I beat myself up night and day about it, my mother took it the worst, dad is found most nights crapulous in his study.

Chad had been going to get me a present for my birthday in haste, inadvertently he forgot to purchase one after he got off work. He was bringing me a new baseball glove when a vehicle ran a stop sign coming into Carlton at an intersection and slammed into his car. His body was found on the hood, blood painted the image in my mind forever like a Jackson Pollock.

I missed the next shot on purpose. May glared at me, "Are you going easy?"

"No, I was distracted as you waltzed by." Which in part was true, though I could make a shot left handed with my eyes shut if I felt the need.

Pulling out a cigarette, I offered her one, we smoked, she moved around the table like a pinball machine and wiped me out in one turn. First woman that ever played 8-ball at par with me. I challenged her to another match and three more after that. Winning our tournament by the skin of my teeth, she tittered like a woman accustomed to sharking a man.

"You scratched on the 8-ball intentionally?" Tapping ash in a packed-to-the-brim tray, her eyes green as the bottled glass I saw my dashing reflection in.

"No more than you missed your shot." She winked.

After a half hour more of conversing, mulling over details, Maybelline wrote her address down on a bar napkin with cherry blossom pink lipstick, asked if I would write to her sometime, said I would if she didn't mention her crushing my dignity at a game of billiards. I watched her with a drunken gaze as she sauntered out of the threshold, losing my breath for a moment. The bar grew dingy as her light faded into the street, Abe came over with Josiah, baring inquisitive indentations in their foreheads as they squinted at me.

"You alright, Hank?" Abe looked me over as if my face were blue.

"Cat got your tongue?" Josiah spoke to my surprise.

Unabashedly, I told them, "I am in heaven," holding up a lip-stick-painted napkin with art worth every penny as much as Leonardo's Mona Lisa, "and you thought my tie and watch would frighten her." We cackled like hyenas as I carefully folded the napkin to insert in my pocket.

"Well done," Abe had a cigar bobbing as he spoke, "If you're done dawdling over here, me and Josiah would like to get going, 12:30 already."

"Fine, there's a bottle of rum on ice at my place." I wish I could have bought one more dram for my new friends. Heading out the door, I lead the way to my apartment, past the post office on the right, a few minutes walk from here.

We never made it.

3

A crescent moon illuminated our walk, save a few sections where a towering alder blocked out a stretch of five feet. The bell from its perch atop the Baptist church nearing my abode left the path ahead of us black as night. The conversationalist I was, I did the majority of the talking, most of it about Maybelline. There was an occasion when Josiah would tell a joke, he was a rather humorous character for the scary giant he appeared to be. Abe pulled out a flask of bourbon and passed it my way.

"This safe to drink?" Had to know, the grin on Abe's face was questionable.

"It might collapse a lung–or two." Dry humor, rarity in this town. I took a swig, to be fair, it was better than I anticipated, though potent as it was I choked, my eyes began to water, the sheen of a crescent moon transmuted through dilated pupils.

"Pass it here," Josiah demanded. He took a pull from it like it was water.

"Get on the ground!" I heard from behind, the hammer of a revolver being cocked. Annoyed, I figured it was the cops harassing us. When the three of us turned around, I counted seven brawny men with pantyhose masking their faces, the stench of alcohol more prevalent in the air as it radiated from our assailants.

"Listen," I said, hands held cautiously in the air, "we are going that way," pointing with my thumb backwards, "we don't want any trouble." I

14

dropped my hands back down, they were not police and they did not tell me to raise them again.

"Give us your money!" The man holding the gun bellowed.

Josiah is a sentimental individual. His money was earned through hard, intensive, laborious work, laboring in the sun for sixty-five cents an hour with no overtime. "Like hell, I recommend you walk away," hostility sewed into each phrase.

"Larson?" I recognized his nasal tone, the size of the men with him, I had no doubt these were our colleagues present, hot to trot for a reprisal.

Revealing his face, a revolver primed and aimed at Abe, "Boys take the masks off," I was right. "Give us your money, don't put up a fight, take a beating and we will be on our way." I took off my newsboy cap, holding it ready in my hand, the razor blades fitting at the back shined with malice. Next to where I kept my smokes in the front pocket of my blazer I had my hand fondling a butterfly knife. I had learned early on to always be prepared.

"Walk away." Abe warned. The men got closer. Stored in Abe's back pocket was a sap, two men approached, quick as the devil he pelted them on the forehead and jumped to evade the shot Larson fired.

"Abe!" Josiah furious. Three shots embedded into Abe's gut, he fell back gasping for air like a woman giving birth. We had all drunk heavily, thinned blood was not in our favor. Restraint was in Josiah's blood until his brother was shot. See, he had no weapons, he never needed any with stupendous fists that smashed like anvils. More shots went off, three of the seven men stayed back, one was at my side with a skinning knife, without hesitation I swung with my cap clipping chin and lunged with a scalpel-sharp butterfly knife slitting throat, liquid poured from four snipped jugular veins, blood masqueraded as my hand, piping hot, this was getting nasty quick. Frankly, I was in shock. That was the first man I had ever killed.

The rest of the men scattered, Josiah was pummeling what was left of Larson's face into pulp, a gruesome macabre sight. I had a foreboding feeling as I went to Abe's aid, there was blood encompassing his still form like a puddle, I put my hand behind his neck to brace his head like a newborn, looking into his eyes I saw relief, and he passed. A man has the right to cry, so I did, a lesser man would not admit that.

Eyes cast down at Abe, I closed his eyelids as tears spider-webbed my cheeks. "Josiah!" I squalled, "Abe! He is gone..." Sirens in the distance, someone must have called it in, we managed not to cause a ruckus at the bar, here was a different story.

Rising to my feet, Josiah was not speaking, I looked to see him lying next to Larson's corpse, I feared for the worst, running over, what I saw I almost could not believe. Josiah's body was riddled with bullets, one went into his lung I could hear him wheezing, drowning in his own blood, I knelt down next to him and cursed the gods. Blood, so much, I tried to stop it with worthless hands.

"It's ... okay," Josiah, fighting off internal bleeding and the torrent of asphyxia for as long as he could.

"Shh ... Shh ... Don't speak, the cops are coming, you'll be alright," I reiterated, "you'll be alright." He coughed, ejected what blood he could, some splattered my face, some did not. I lied to him, this world is not made of miracles in every facet. This time my handkerchief covered a horrified face, I lost a piece of myself. Traumatized, I slumped over and stared at the prepossessing stars simultaneously while holding Josiah's hand as I walked him into the light.

Our altercation, a squabble at the tracks was the cause of this, if I would have stopped, abstained from egging Larson on, maybe all of this could have been prevented.

The stench of copper lingered in the air, overpowering as were my emotions, tears flowed freely like a bird soaring in the ether. Josiah did not say another word as I clenched his hand, from warm to cold I felt the life leave a friend. Words are inadequate for the disreputable sensation I feel, heartbroken, crestfallen, I sunk into the ground below. Abe's flask lay next to me on stained ground, I extended my arm to retrieve it, chugged the contents, my stomach raged in contempt. Pain, I felt pain set in my bones, wrap my intestines, strangle my heart, it felt right as part of me died.

4

Sirens, alarms, the noise was resounding, it bashed at my skull, four dead bodies, four lives that did not have to be sacrificed. Sent to where I do not know. Lost for eternity. Small town cops were aghast, I heard them call for help over the static of a CB, saying that five were found dead. I was, mostly. As I held my dead friend's hand, the cop looked down at me, chest moving intermittently. I was not sure who was in more shock, he or I.

"Oh my god! Luis, come over here! One's alive!" His partner ran over, I was brought to my feet, they checked me for wounds, flummoxed for there was blood coating me and no injury on the surface.

But, the inside, broken.

After a long night at the precinct, I was acquitted of any charges, I murdered a man in self-defense and walked away scot-free except for the ominous cloud that would hang above my head wherever I went now. The story and recollection of events took hours, officers jotting down on paper, I was labeled as a raconteur, honest, despondent, depressed. A list trailed twenty pages, most of which inclined that I should consider a form of psychiatric care. One of the guys frazzled by the night as I brought me a pot of coffee, tears were put on standby, I had a rain check for them when I made it home. In great detail, I covered the case of tonight and the first quarrel working on the train tracks.

The chief was nice enough to slip me some of his private hooch into my extra black coffee that compared to sludge scraped from the bottom of a septic tank. I needed every nerve agent I could get. Killing takes the coldest part of you out, sticks it in your face, and shows you what kind of horrible things you are capable of. In my experience that is. I had few friends as a wee lad, aging thinned out the remainder of those who claimed to be such from school, Abe and his brother Josiah were the closest thing to friends I had in some time. Later I found out the name of the man I murdered: Tod. Whom I cut from ear to ear with my butterfly knife.

Afterwards, I genuinely comprehended Darwinism. I survived ... but at what cost?

My friends died.

Hell comes from within, bred by adverse selection and exhibited in our eyes, a gateway to the soul.

When I left the constable with more paperwork than he had for the last year, he offered to give me a ride home, I passed. Tarnished bloodstained clothes gave off a funny odor as the sun suspended overhead like a spotlight cooked me. Looking at my watch, it was a quarter past twelve, I got home and tossed my knife into the wall from sheer frustration, it stuck and twanged. Without deliberation, I chucked my hat at the counter near the sink, grabbed the bottle of aged rum I was to have shared with Abe and Josiah. Tossing the screw top in my trash bin, I grabbed a 45, first pressing, jazz, dropped the needle and cranked up the volume. Bottle in hand, no glass needed, I sat on a chair at the dining table and began drowning out my thoughts.

5

A week later I attended Abe and Josiah's funeral, it took more guts than I thought I had. Being the only white man there, I stuck out like a sore thumb. The mother of the two spotted me, we connected eyes and shared our misery. I knew she hated me, the anguish and guilt was mine to bear.

I brought two roses, one for each, poured a shot of five dollar whiskey in each of their graves, as the caskets were deposited in their eternal resting places. A queer sight for whoever was watching, I shook a hand filled with dirt from the railroad tracks where we became friends out in each burial pit.

Weeping, melancholy, severance from this life, we were all there to mourn the dead, though I knew they would live on within each and every one of us. Men clad in black suits with gray ties, some wore fedoras, others wore nothing to shade from the sun beating against our backs. Women with pillbox hats atop their heads, veils hung in front of faces, translucent to the eye and did not hide the wave of tears. Prayers were audible, some inaudible, as the casket was lowered, voices shook by tragedy, cracking at the edges. I said a few words myself though they were only selfish–I asked for forgiveness.

Like any good drunk I licked the rim of Abe's flask, eyes downcast at his grave, his mother came up to me. I dared not to look her dead on–shame, nothing but shame and contrition saturated my essence. Out of the sight of my peripherals, she stood there, mouth gaping, for what I only guessed was animosity. I did not blame her, I despised myself to boot. Her veil was moved out of the way of her face as if to make this interaction worse. She was a beautiful coffee-black woman, her age was not shown, thirty-five, maybe forty years old for all I could read. Eyes, two, filled with disgust, shot me like a twelve-gauge. I drank more from her son's flask, heels crunched grass, one step, two step, closer she came. My heart fluctuated like the first time I kissed a girl, except that was out of excitement, this was from a dull butter knife shoved between ribs, metaphorically, though. If it were in actuality, it would not have hurt more than what she said.

"You! You did this!" Her voice rancid in my ears, "You're that boy!" The word boy was a euphemism, she really meant devil. Blaming me would not bring her children back, but if it was the burden she needed to be relieved of, I deserved that much.

"My sons," she cried, eyes wavering between me and their graves, the words barely left her mouth, diluted by sobs, "they were all I had …" I felt fragile like paper-thin glass and she was walking across the top of it heavy-footed.

"Miss, I'm–" She cut me off without hesitation.

"Their father abandoned us when they were born," disturbed eyes looked upon a broken man, "they … were all … I had." Her words were like daggers driven into my coffin, emotion bled from me like a wounded dog yelping.

"They … were … my … friends," I said, heartsick, as if that would make this situation any better.

Turmoil left Abe and Josiah's mom dejected, every friend, family member, and acquaintance looked my way as if I were Satan himself. "You! How dare you!" She came closer, her voice reverberated end-to-end of the cemetery, my skin had goosebumps, concealed only by fabric.

"Friends don't get other friends dead!" Her fists walloped my chest for all it was worth, like a rug beater and I a bedraggled rug, she left me black and blue. Lungs stifled, I could not feel pain from the outside, the imbalance within alone was overwhelming.

"I swear I didn't mean to!" I whimpered, she could not cause me more harm than I had already done to myself.

To tell the truth, I had tried earlier to hang myself in the bathroom by electrical cord and a pipe protruding from the wall, after a minute the pipe broke from my weight. Water cascaded to the ground, I slipped as I fell, between life and death, I awoke to my shortcomings. My landlord assumed it was due to happen any time, old pipes burst. The marks of my failure were hidden beneath the collar of my cotton dress shirt.

The harm we do to ourselves is more nocuous than what another human being could possibly do.

"You killed them!" She smacked me in the jaw with each gloved hand. "Their death is on your hands!"

The deceased's close family came to my assistance, alarmed, dragging Josiah's mom back, one brute of a man on each arm as she flailed, heels dug a rut in the earth, I dropped to my knees and beat my fists into the ground until my knuckles split, blood gleamed, dead, they were dead.

Alcohol slightly soothed shaky hands, sweaty palms soaked the front of my trousers as I picked myself back up. If I didn't, nobody else would. I was unwelcome here, atrocious in their eyes. I was not the one to shoot either of her sons, I loaded the gun so to speak, but Larson fired. Him being dead and all left me to carry what felt like the weight of the world on my shoulders. Pulling out a cigarette, I stood next to tombstones with names of men I barely got to know, hardworking brothers with bodies the Greeks would have sculpted. Minds as simple and straightforward as average men, smiles as pretty as any ladies', good people, they truly were.

Everyone vacated the premises, I stood there sweating in the sun, ripped through an entire pack of cigarettes in little over a few hours. Day turned to night, rain washed the ground, encouraging grass to grow. I tore into a pack of cheap cigars and left one on each headstone for my friends as a parting gift.

I walked away and never looked back.

6

A rambling man:
I walked through the night, I had no car and the cemetery was miles from my dwelling. Out of cigarettes, I should have brought a bottle of whiskey, my lungs hated me from all the tobacco smoke. I hated me too, the three cigars left in the pack were indulged, lightheaded from inhaling, I swore ghosts were coming out of the darkness. Haunting me, my brother, then Abe and Josiah, they all were playing tricks on my mind.

This went on until I reached Carlton. Clothes drenched, down and out, and needing someone to talk to. I grabbed the rest of my five dollar bottle from the ice box and headed back out the door with an address written on a piece of paper.

Sad to say, I had already put my parents through enough, so I did not head down Kutch Street, where my mom was probably staring hopelessly in the dark at memories from her past. Smoke billowed around her as she exhaled, dad in his study drinking scotch, looking over documents and puffing on a Cuban. No, I did not bother them. They were long gone, my appearance there would only make things worse.

At the door, I checked my watch, tapped on her door. I heard a switch flicked. The light came on and footsteps scurried to the front door. Waiting patiently, I played with a new pack of cigarettes in my pocket.

May opened her apartment door, she looked at me and I at her, I could tell she sensed something wrong. That, or she already knew.

"Hank?"

"May, you mind if I come in? I need someone to talk to, listen I know it's–" She grabbed my ice cold hands, pulled me in. I dripped like a drenched dog, had a bottle of whiskey angling out of my pocket, if you did not see a sad case–you had to be blind.

We sat down in her kitchen, I took my jacket off, apologized for getting anything wet. She removed the newspaper away from where it covered an antique half-round folding banquet table with a spotty white top up against the wall beneath a window. Putting my cigarettes on the table, I opened the pack and propped it up next to the ashtray, offering her one. Maybelline sat across me with a worried expression my mother always had. We smoked for a spell in silence, thoughts drifting around us, I watched her with grief-stricken eyes.

"You never wrote …"

If I could have smiled then, I would have. She placed two wide-based glasses tapered to a narrow top down next to my bottle. I recognized the nosing glass made for whiskey. Generously I poured two shots in each, and we drank. She slid her glass back to me. I streamed another shot in each. This time we took it slow as we sipped before speaking.

"I know … look I really had a good time with you at the pub … it's just …" I took a drag from my cigarette and tapped the ember out in her ashtray.

"Hank, I know. I heard … saw," she gulped saliva down like it was a weight in her throat, "the paper was delivered here three days ago … god how awful," May stared into my eyes.

I am not sure what she saw within as we soul-gazed.

"It–we were ambushed after we left the bar." Words stuck in my throat as I forced them out, "We were friends … we worked together." In frustration, I made fists with both hands and squeezed them tight as I could, the blood walking away from my knuckles.

She ashed her cigarette, "How, horrible … I heard gunshots from here, my window was cracked because of the heat. I was scared," May was panicked, "I didn't know what was going on." Her green eyes never faltered from mine. Normally I would have felt unease, but I found comfort in her gaze. Dealing out another double, we clinked glasses as a toast to Abe and Josiah. Brothers.

"Larson, pigheaded," I paused, it was not proper to speak ill of the dead but, he caused me a great deal of strife, "shot them dead, tried to mug us—was all my fault." I buried my face in my hands as elbows were propped against the tabletop.

Ambivalently, she turned her head back and forth. "No ... no it couldn't have been your fault, Hank." It was, more than she could have possibly known.

"May, I provoked those men earlier at work. They were saying racial terms, I wouldn't stand by. My mouth ran faster than my mind, I knew better."

She took a nip from her glass. I was drunk. She grabbed another smoke and lit it with a flimsy match. With a subtle twist of her wrist, the match was quashed.

"What it sounds like is you were defending them. Any man would be proud of what you did. No one could have foreseen," her voice was smooth as chamomile tea, "that Larson and his group would have come after you with a gun."

Thinking of him makes me sick. I can still imagine his face caved in by Josiah's fists as he avenged his brother.

"But ... but..."

"Hank, don't do this to yourself."

Grabbing a cigarette, I shook my head as the flame from a match licked the tip. "I just ... I don't know how to cope. Even when my brother died, I locked myself away in a metaphoric vault with a code nobody could decipher." I had let that slip: mentioning my brother's death at the bar when I referred to playing pool frequently with him growing up.

I never disclosed that he was torn from this world.

She asked about my brother Chad, I told her the story. I tried not to cry, her hands met mine, we drank some more. Our fingers weaved after she scooted her chair beside me, the linoleum floor squeaked in retort.

I made her cry. I am not sure if it was mostly due to the liquor or my stories. Incredulously, she looked upon me as if I were a wounded dog, I straightened my back and took a deep inhalation of stagnant, smokey air.

The events made me feel like a coward. My pride was pissed on. I was internally broken. And, my sovereignty was all there was left to glue the pieces back together.

One sliver at a time.

Her lips were pressed against mine—soft, sweet, kind. Our hearts skipped a beat. My hand went of its own volition to the back of her head, where hair covered it as I held her close to me. Maybelline grabbed my hand, drunk and poor for movement. She guided it to her waist where it lifted her blouse and rested at the curve of her hip. We twisted tongues, intimate, hot, sedate. We kissed like immortals, time was a word we never understood. In my stupor, I bumped the empty bottle of whiskey with an elbow, she acted as if it never happened.

We separated mouths for only a moment as she said, "Your clothes, they're soaked," she started to loosen my tie. "Let's get them off so you don't catch a cold."

That was fine with me—then I realized—I forgot something.

"Your neck ... those marks." May massaged my throat with delicate fingers, as if not to irritate the skin anymore, "oh ... you ... I am so sorry."

She hadn't done anything wrong. May had no reason to feel sorry, nor pity me. Perturbed, she wept. I felt hollow and mortified, though May did not stop taking my clothes off. She knew why the marks were there, I never had to confide in her that dark secret.

My shirt came off, she fondled my muscles. From my arms to my abdomen, my back, then to my rugged face. Never had I been with a woman before. I was a novice, but everything felt so natural—intuitively we carried on through the process. I picked her up and brought her to the couch in her small living room, my khakis came off next, buckle undone, then I was sitting with her atop me just in skivvies. Breath warm, blown against my neck as I undid the clips at the back of her brassiere like an amateur ... a puzzle I lacked experience with. After moments, her chest was bare, then her lower half—we were both naked.

"Wait ... Maybelline," I said before we could progress any further.

"What ...?" Ecstasy escaped her lungs to form words that tickled my skin.

"It's not ... right–will you be my girlfriend?" My voice sounded startled, I had no intentions of getting with a woman that was not mine. I had old values discarded by later generations.

"Ye ... sss," she hissed like a snake in my ear before biting my lip.

7

May and I had passion, made love on the couch in her apartment for the first time. Maybelline became my girlfriend, lover, and best friend. Over the years we grew close as any, after the first time we fornicated I moved into her apartment. She begged me … my suitcase and luggage was packed within an hour. Statistics say cohabiting before marriage will result in an early divorce in most cases. Collectively, we said the hell with it.

Cherishing every waking, hot air blown into my ear before a kiss in the morning, her chest placed against mine, frantic for breath. I'd be out like a light before she knew it, still drunk or hungover most times. The past remained where it ineluctably does. Alcohol and Maybelline came in handy when hindsight left me disordered. Our love was toasted. Drinks were had. Long romantic evenings. We danced on Monday night like crazed lovers in the kitchen to the sound of a record player circling the grooves of an old record.

May taught me a thing or two about swing, I showed her waltz. Periodically, on Friday and Saturday nights, we went out to a local dance hall where the drinks were always cold, the ambiance was pleasant, and hips twisted and turned until the moon went down.

8

When I went back to the train tracks for work after an excused absence for bereavement, there were empty spots to fill. After some time, my boss hired another four men and, within a couple years, we successfully linked the towns together. Not at any time did I forget what went on all those years ago. At my request, a plaque was engraved with Abe and Josiah's faces and names, respects were written below. In light of a better day, I wrote:

"Save a spot for me one day when my work is through, part the clouds and pour me a glass, light me a cigarette, we will have a lot of catching up to do."

Their mom thanked me with a letter and gave me a sun-faded black and white photo of her sons. She on no account forgave me—I did not expect her to. The cold truth of it all still had me unsettled. Their deaths will rest on my hands, along with the man whose throat I slashed in desperation for my own survival. Days and nights will come and go, but the cold fact still remains. History cannot be wiped clean, just as the record books stay the same, so do the memories prodding my psyche. To become a better man, to develop, to alter the future, those are the attempts I will make in order to ensure a life for me yet to live. Ambitions are the difference between me and that of a lesser man. Ambitions are what will guide me through the cold days of winter and the scorching ones of summer.

To pay my respects in a final attempt, I will live on for Abe and Josiah. - *Until we meet again.*

With work being through at the station, there were no available positions operating the locomotives, to my annoyance, I searched for a job. Countless nights were spent searching for work, smoking through packs of cigarettes from anxiety that wouldn't subside. Maybelline continued working at the bank, we shared everything without question. To her suggestion, I had a sum of money saved at the bank in town. Unfortunately, it was decreasing with passing weeks.

I applied to innumerable establishments for work, no one was hiring and, if they were, my experience on the track did not amount to much. You know you have a drinking problem when your neighbor's garbage can is where you divide the empty bottles into. May and I both drank heavily those days, it was a luxury not to be missed. There was a point where I was truly destitute, money ran out in my account, save for a few nickels and a buck. Enough for minimal groceries and not even close for a car to drive for work.

Mother and father were retired and living off of funds they could not part with. Each had a drinking problem after my brother died on my birthday, each smoked heavily, and property taxes were not cheap. Maybelline earned a raise while I was searching for work, up from seventy to seventy-five cents.

One day May came home after work, about five-thirty, I had just scoured the paper for any sign of a job that would accept me. She had bags under her eyes, tired from the day's exertion. Counting bills and coins can leave your eyes imagining money you don't have. Her hair was done up in a bun I had helped her with that morning, red lipstick, light makeup on her cheeks.

"News, I have news, honey, " she slammed the door. Disturbing the individuals around the block, scaring a tomcat from his perch on a picket fence as he eyed down hummingbirds feeding at the feeder I had placed out last week. Her excitement was worth all the racket.

"Yes," I said, thinking as if the stars aligned, "what might it be? Here, let me grab your coat." Grabbing her coat and hanging it by the hook near the door, she leaned for a customary kiss after work. Lips sweet as caramel candy—at times I was afraid my teeth would rot from all the sweetness.

"Delilah," she paused to wipe rose-colored lipstick from my face, "there is a job," breath escaping her lungs with joy, "start Monday."

I was having trouble deciphering it all with her choppy speech. "Who's Delilah?" I asked.

"She is that lassie from the bank: blonde hair, blue eyes, short bob cut, wears denim frequently?" I looked at her confused as she spoke of the woman, a language of subtle cues from clothes, eye color, hair, etc.

"Hank, the one I speak of quite often. The one I am fond of," she looked at me, searching for a response while I was still dumbfounded. "She's nice and wants to go out for drinks tonight." Friday night, drink—I could go for that. And, if this lady was proposing a job, maybe it might be my niche.

"Are you talking about the one whose husband is a car salesman in McMinnville at the Ford dealership?" I could speak cars, most men could. Far as a mechanic went, I was not talented in the slightest. May walked to work, I used to before I was laid off. With nothing to fix, there was nothing to learn from hands on.

Books are only good for half the battle.

She sat down on the sofa to take off her heels and place them by the door, I put a cigarette in her mouth and got the cherry going with a reusable metal lighter I received from the train station for my service. Engraved on one side was my first and last name, on the opposite side it had an ornate locomotive, tracks and the station. Classy gift I approved of, it was the least they could do after laying me off.

Exhaling a cloud of smoke in my face, she said, "Sorry just aflutter, Hank. This could be it, a career, and yes, that's the one."

Returning the elation, I smiled and told her, "It's a start, nothing is set in stone. What time would we perhaps go have a drink with these folk?"

"Her husband, Damon, gets off work at six, and she said they would eat supper. Close to eight-thirty?" She asked as if the time would work for me. I had nothing else going on like normal. Most nights were spent reading and seldom would I write. Drinking spirits was a given.

"Which tavern is our rendezvous, or are we going dancing?" Already walking to the kitchen for a drink of twenty-cent vodka, I knew the answer before she even said it. I was leaning against the wall while she smoked on the sofa, dabbing her cigarette in the ashtray. That was before the past came back to me like a tidal wave and I was submerged, no oxygen–I needed air.

"The pub here in town, Hank …" I cracked the window, cold air blew in against my clean-shaven face. "Listen, I know–" Abruptly, I stopped her from finishing.

"You know how I feel about it, May. That place is a nightmare for me." Eyelids squinted, I gazed into a crystal glass with hundred-proof liquid, knocked it back, coughed, a tear dropped to the floor.

"Listen, will you, dammit," May was cute when she cursed, her jaw set, "Look at it from this perspective, will you. We met there … I found you and you found me. Something good came of that night, if only that one thing … me." Her thumb hooked back pointing at a dimple. I walked over and offered her a nip from my glass, she finished the rest before I could snatch it back.

"You are right." Women normally are, and if they are not, agree with them anyways. Words from the wise. "Hey, look at me." She had her eyes cast at the floor, living my nightmare, the sickness that was still haunting me most days.

"What–" I laid another kiss on her juicy red lips, we worked our way back to the bedroom where a queen-sized mattress with plaid wool sheets hid a surprise beneath. Dropping down to my rear end on the side as not to disrupt the delicate gift in wait.

Her legs and arms wrapped around me like a good old-fashioned bearhug, she had my tie off and was working the front buttons loose of my black dress shirt. Simultaneously, I undid her bun and let her hair down to her shoulders. Our mouths never separated in fear that we might die, though dying in the middle of the hot mess this was to be did not sound a terrible way to kick the bucket.

"May ..." my words were deep and scratchy, as my voice had problems with pitch in the heat of the moment.

Her dimples were present as she smiled, thinking I was teasing her again. "What sweetheart?"

Behind my back, slick as the devil, I pulled out a bouquet of roses I spent the last of the money I had in the bank on. Food was important, but this, this was imperative.

"Happy anniversary." Three years had gone by in the blink of an eye, we lived in the same apartment she had back when we first met. I treated her with the same amount of passion and intensity as when we first became lovers, if not more now.

"Awwwww ..." Tears came to her eyes, I wiped them away as lightly as I could with thumbs as rough as eighty-grit sandpaper. I knew not only was the good news she brought home truth, but a distraction. To be honest, I hear most women test their man, well, I've not been known to fail before. Expectantly, when she kissed me at the door, I knew May was waiting for me to say it.

I had to tantalize her first.

"You ... remembered!" Her hug was solace, bliss, happily ever after. She squeezed me to death and some, her little arms had trouble, but she managed. "I love you!" Ecstatically, her words of rapture spoken in a high-pitched caterwaul in my ear, deafening me for a moment.

"And I love you. I love you Maybelline." Our lips met again. I fell to my back and May held her flowers, sniffing them. I smiled, the astonishment would not be over quite yet.

My mother gave me a gift when I stopped by last, she said I deserved it. Of course, after mentioning everything I had been through in the past, telling me I really earned something good: Maybelline and my grandmother's ring, that is. Naturally, it was supposed to be given to my older brother, but, since he passed, I was the one to collect. A silver band with a diamond the size of a worn down marble kids played with to their heart's content. It was grand to say the least, but not as grand as my girlfriend's expression.

Maybelline had been distracted by the bouquet, and when she noticed

32

a letter folded around an item, she had the most peculiar look. Pulling out the real surprise of the evening, she set the roses down to the side of the bed on top of a stack of books I had haphazardly lain across our nightstand. Skeptically, she eyed me, wondering what sort of trickery I was up to this time. Proceeding to unfold the letter, May dashed her eyes back at me, covering my smile with a weather-cracked hand then back to the letter, a ring fell out and dropped to my chest, she didn't notice.

The letter read in semi-legible handwriting: "To A Love That Never Dies."

With cool ease, I snatched the ring off my chest, picked her up as tears released like floodgates at the Hoover Dam. Placing her rump on the bed to spectate, swiftly I dropped down on one knee, tie missing, shirt halfway unbuttoned, sloppy, tousled hair–I proposed.

"May ... Maybelline," she sat on the bed crying with her head tilted down, I used my pointer finger to raise her chin up, looked her in the eyes, "I want to spend the rest of my life with you ... even when we are ghosts ... I want to be ... with you."

At this moment, chivalry got the best of me like normal, pulling out a checkered handkerchief, I dabbed at her face. I was nervous, but I continued, "Will you take my hand in marriage and be–my wife?"

"Oh ... Hank!" The ring was held out to where she could see it, her hand extended. I placed it on her ring finger.

"Yes! Yes! Of course! In a million lives. Every time. Yes!" May stopped crying, she hopped from the bed and onto my chest like I was prey she was ready to kill. The door to our room was close by and I smacked my head on it as she pushed me down to the carpet.

Never had I been so happy in my life, when the girl of my dreams said yes. So much emotion was poured into the touch of lips and tongue, she bit me good, lips, earlobe, neck. I had my hands all over her body while she was on top. Taking her clothes off with practiced hands, sober too at the moment, if I might add. Drunk on love, she ripped the rest of my shirt open and off, buttons flew–her superpowers with needle and thread would come into use at a later date when we were not as preoccupied.

Proudly, she rested her head and arms across my chest, we never made it back to the bed. I fished a smoke out of my pants pocket, tapping the butt against my index finger's knuckle, I packed it, lit, and handed it to May. We spoke for a while, dreams of the future, trips, vacations we would like to take, where we would move to. Carlton was my stomping grounds, as silly as it sounds, she enjoyed the tranquility of the area. Together we agreed on a secluded place on the outskirts when an opportune moment came floating our way.

Far as dinner went, we skipped it. Cracking a new bottle open of twenty-cent vodka, tasted like rubbing alcohol, but, man was it good–potent, but good. We sat in the kitchen, I had the light off and a candle going at the table. Jazz played in the background, smooth, crisp, subtle. We relished our anniversary, it was nearing 8 p.m. and we almost forgot after all the excitement.

"You said your friend from work and her husband were going to be at the bar around–"

"8:30–shoot." She broke from the table, glass in hand. I chuckled, sipped ambrosia, and followed her to the room to get ready.

"So, this husband of hers, is he something special?"

"Average fellow from what Delilah said; works in sales, does considerably well. Drives a Model A. Navy blue. Drinks–smokes Cubans like your father," she said dispassionately, as if it did not matter and she had other things on her mind.

May was sitting in front of a baroque mirror, leaning forward doing her eyeliner. I was smoking a cigarette, already dressed and ready. She took her time. It didn't bother me, I was drinking until my skin numbed, drunk as a skunk. "Yeah, but is he a gentleman?" If he treated women right, I could respect him.

May was plucking a hair, "From what I heard, sharp guy, kind, treats his wife right."

"Good, good to hear. So the job, he might be able to assist?" Eyebrows raised, hopeful, the way May slammed the door earlier I knew it had to be positive.

"She said he was needing a man for sales. A position opened up after a guy ran amok," pausing to apply more red lipstick after smooching the life out of me incidentally removed most of it, "had to be bedridden for too long, so they fired him."

"My time to shine," I winked at her.

Laughing for all it was worth, she said, "Play on words there, Mr. Shine?"

"And soon to be Mrs. Shine," winking again at my beloved. She finished decorating her already blemish-free face and kissed me. Conjointly, we walked out the door after I topped off an old friend's flask for good luck.

9

We were used to walking everywhere. People had cars, although legs were free of charge and did not require insurance, or gasoline. In some sense, we were saving money as we held hands all the way to the pub. It had been three years or more since I went there, time fades like the echo of a gunshot. Within minutes, I was opening the door for my lady and the smokey bar served as our shelter for the evening. Not a single change in aesthetic, welcoming us back like it was just yesterday that the tragedy transpired.

Making eye contact with the bartender, he wrinkled his forehead like he knew me. The same mustache-twirled character worked behind the bar, with sweaty palms and tips shoved into his apron. "What'll you 'ave, sonny?" he said as I walked up.

"Take an old-fashioned, mint julep for the lassie." I scrounge for change in my pocket, my wallet was dust and had spiderwebs when I opened it.

Sending a dollar his way, one I had stashed in a book as a marker. He said with a cigar waving up and down as he spoke, "Don't worry about it lad, saw the paper a few years back, can't forget your face. Drinks are on the house for you and her." Sliding the glasses forward, he grinned a mental patient grin.

"Thank you, sir, appreciate it, really do." Regardless of the free drink, I left the money it would have cost me on the bar top.

"That was nice," Maybelline said as we walked over to the back, where a booth adjoined the pool table I was so fond of, had been some time since I played last. May looked at me for challenge, shaking her head, wordlessly mouthing "boys and their games."

"Sure was, free drinks, don't make yourself sick. And keep it down, wouldn't want your friend to question me about why." May nodded, I took her jacket off and she mine, brought them over to a rack to hang them and then sat down.

"Should be here any moment." She crossed her legs, I clasped my drink and took a deep sip to fight off the nerves this place was stirring up in me.

"Hope so, let's keep the proposal under lock and key as well." She understood, May can read me like an open book. I said what I said because I was not trying to be some salesman's pity case and have him flick me a job like a penny to a vagrant.

"Alright Hank, relax now—I love you." Her subtle voice reassuring, like a dream, this was all surreal. Odd how you look back on your life and in such a short time everything can change, I was only twenty-two, but, damn, did I feel old.

After our second round of drinks at 8:55, they finally showed up. Stopping at the bar, Delilah whom I presumed as she was waving to Maybelline with red gloves, adorned with a cute red blouse and a white scarf strangling her neck as I saw her fight for air, either that or the magnanimous bartender's smoke he blew in her face. For all I knew, the man owned the joint and could do whatever the hell he wanted. Her husband, who I am troubled to recall his name, eyed over. He was older than her, probably forty-five and she was about thirty. His hair was red. His shoes cost him more than I made in a month. His tie was two-toned with black and white stripes, and the blazer he wore was black with a white shirt on underneath. He was sharp, no doubt about that. Where I had a seven dollar watch, his Rolex cost a boatload.

"Your friend, right?" May grabbed my hand.

"Yeah, that's her, she's lovely, isn't she?" She was, pretty girl.

Standing up, I shook Delilah's hand, then her husband's. May hugged her friend like they were sisters separated since birth, even though it had only been five hours or so. Women are like that generally–expressive.

"Name's Hank, Hank Shine." Firm grip, you can tell a lot about a man by the way he shakes your hand. I could tell he worked sales, my hands were rough as gravel, his were soft.

"Damon Parrish, nice to meet you," his voice was hard as stone, direct, used to getting what he wanted. I matched him.

"Pleasure. May said your wife was a real sweetheart?" Snagging my glass off the table, took a sip while I speculatively listened to him speak.

"Ah, Delilah–to the core. We've been married for five years, love her like a deathwish. Nothing more I could ask, she'll make you laugh too." He nodded at me. I nodded in turn. May and Delilah walked over to the jukebox to select music, talk gal stuff, the usual.

"That's good to hear, congrats." Bored with standing, we sat down on red leather, the booth was classy, from the Victorian era.

"Smoke?" I had my pack out, flicked the bottom to send one out an inch for casual removal.

"Why not," he withdrew it, "thanks." I lit mine then handed him my lighter. "No thanks, have my own." Bringing forth a gold reusable lighter.

Mine was silver, no big deal, I shrugged.

"May said your wife mentioned something about a sales job starting Monday?" Damon's eyes were the color of worn copper pennies.

"Well, to tell you the truth, it's a funny story." This sounded misleading, to my displeasure, I crossed the fingers of my right hand under the table, held my cigarette with my left.

"Do tell." With a fake half-drawn smile, I grabbed my glass and drank, turned my neck to see the ladies talking over a record being dropped. Classical music played, I enjoy Bach myself. At a bar, jazz was the way to go. Girls have different tastes evidently.

"Well," he flicked the ash on the ground as if the tray was not good enough, the guy serving drinks looked over at us with scorn, "Randy, he went out last week and made an ass of himself. Broke a few bottles at the bar in McMinnville down Third Street, tried to stab an older gentleman for bumping into him more than once that night. Randy had his jaw broken, two ribs, and all the fingers on his left hand. Afraid sales won't work for him anymore." Mulling over the idiocy of Randy, I dragged from a flattened butt squished by clammy fingers.

He said with sophistication, "The boss won't accept that," taking a lungful of smoke, wheezing, then continuing, "makes the company look bad. Drunk and disorderly, injured like he was in a plane crash. No, we can't have that. This opportunity is yours, if you are interested?" His fingers were laced, eyes looking over, curious for what I might say.

"Randy," sipping on a whiskey sour, I said, "real wild card. Straight to the point, I respect that," he nodded solemnly, "the offer sounds appealing ..." Damon should've seen this one coming a mile away, being a salesman and all.

"But?" Astonished as if I were anticipated to jump and dive on the deal. May would have pinched my arm for toying with the man.

Deals are made not by the first offer, but the final.

"See, I can sell cars, I was born to do it." Which was a load of crap, I was winging this as I went. "Making coffee for everyone in the office ... not my forte." He was grinning like a Cheshire cat, he could see a sale coming. "I'll make a bonus, right?" I lit another cigarette, taking a puff and blowing it to the side as I wheezed.

"Yes, substantial at times."

Just what I wanted to hear.

"Fair, add fifty bucks a month to my salary, I want whatever Randy was making as well before he lost his way and decided to falter in public." What Randy made, I don't know. I was willing to bet it was more than I made at the track, plus fifty bucks wouldn't hurt.

Damon had his eyelids tucked back, biting his upper lip in thought. "Forty and you have to make the coffee on Thursday, we all take turns." That I could live with, making the coffee was not a problem when forty dollars were added to the pot.

"His clients, I want them to get started." My vision was that of an alpha, we stared at each other as I smoked to the filter.

"You're a gunner, Hank, I like that. We have a deal, next round's on

you–Monday, be there by eight at the dealership in Mac, Ford, got it?"
Drinks were free for me, so why not, nothing to haggle about.

"Alright, shake on it." We gripped hands, fierce, the ladies came back
over to our booth, smoking and drinking like sailors, giggling, May
blushed at me.

"Sit down, I got your drink," I held it so she did not spill it, we were
both three sheets to the wind prior to arriving here. Drinks on the house,
I was destined to have a hangover I'd never forget.

"So, what were you boys talking about over here?" Delilah asked, her
gaze directed towards me, I looked over at Damon, he cut the back off a
Cuban with a fancy handheld guillotine made of gold. When he sent it
my way, I smiled like a drunkard.

"Thanks, Damon. Delilah, we just were speaking business." I winked
to May as she rested her hand on my leg, I lit the cigar, closed my lighter
with a flick of the wrist and blew O-rings out into the atmosphere.

"And?" May said urgently in response.

"Came to an agreement, Hank Shine is officially starting Monday,"
Damon funneled smoke through each of his nostrils like a dragon
as he spoke.

For the umpteenth time tonight, Maybelline shed a tear for joy, I
wiped it clean and kissed her in front of everyone to see. Every chance I
get to make her smile, my heart beats faster, chest heavy, focus narrowed.
I told May I would be back in a moment, went to the restroom, took a
leak, washed my hands. Startling me as I was still puffing on the cigar and
drying off my hands, Damon came in.

"Hey, you are a hard worker from what Maybeline said. Here, my
treat." Apparently the cigar was not the only thing from Cuba he had. I
knew Coke had it in their soda, but far as snorting it went, I was a novice.

"What the hell, right?" Intoxicated beyond belief, I never thought of
the consequences.

"Here, put your hand out." I did, he had a small vile, tapped a line on
my hand, passed me a twenty dollar bill already rolled. "A bump, that's
all." He was a hell of a salesman, I had a feeling this was not the best
choice to make, but, then again, not the worst either.

Clearing the line off via nostril, it burned, a sensation hard to pin the tail on. I did start to ask myself why I had not tried this before: money was tight and this was an executive's drug. A flame started to burn behind my eyes, stab at my brain—then numb. Adrenaline coursed through me, I felt righteous and on top of the world, president of the United States, a millionaire, like I went from a peasant to a king in a matter of seconds.

"Good, right?" Damon railed a line twice that of mine after prodding me with his elbow, as if we were buddies abruptly.

"Amazing." Drunk, high, relieved, if I was tired a minute ago, now I was wide awake. Drinking too much coffee did not even compare marginally, I heard using a parachute gave you one hell of a jolt, that's what this was: a jolt.

Walking out of the privy, I headed to the bar and ordered another round. With two handfuls of drinks, hyped off cocaine, and trying not to spill. I sat down jittery next to May.

"Are you alright, Hank?" Her eyes slit my veins around the cuff, interrogating, wondering.

"Fine, better than fine," I said with enthusiasm from the core, "Fantastic!" I shouted and kissed her. "Drinks, enjoy every single drop, friends." A shaky hand holding my own glass now consecutively clinked each glass in toast. Delilah batted eyes at me, mirth, same with that of Damon, we were all jazzed, save Maybelline, who had no notion of what was going on.

May looked at me curiously, "Hank, let's go have a cigarette outside," she turned to my new co-worker and hers. "Excuse us for a moment."

Caught so soon, damn.

There was a backdoor, black with a battered bronze door handle, a rug beneath my feet bunched at the end, preventing me from opening said door, I smoothed it out with a jittery right foot like I had to pee real bad, proceeded to open the door and followed May out. She seemed perturbed, drunk, but worried, in fear of her partner, me. If Maybelline was mad, I did not see it, she concealed it well like a tiddly hooker's pistol.

Looking up at the stars, as she said to me gravely, "Hank, your pupils, they're dilated." Hands shook my shoulders out of concern.

DIARY OF A DEAD MAN

"Listen, May," I was lighting her cigarette, then mine. I grabbed both her hands as if the news was daunting, smoke held to the side so she could see the white of my teeth gleam in the moonlight. "Damon offered me a line of cocaine, I accepted." Had I, it felt like my brain had been rolled in shattered glass and I sniffed cinnamon, peculiar, though it felt splendid.

Her jaw went slack, I bit my tongue, devastated. "And you did not think to share?" Astounded, I spun her in a circle like I had many times before on glossy wood dance floors.

Whistling, I said, "Dodged a bullet there. I know, we share everything. Absentmindedness, I forgot, and we were in the bathroom," I mentioned as if to justify, the location was the reason she had not been included. It is better to come clean. Keeping secrets typically stabs you in the back sooner or later, saves you the stress of getting busted too if you just get it over and done with. One quality about me Maybelline loved more than others she confided in me saying "a forthright man is a handsome one, sexy, and dashing in his own individuality", of course, she revealed that after one too many margaritas a night months past.

"Not entirely, the bullet that is. When we get back, ask if I can try a little." May nudged me with her elbow, cute as they come, her black hair fell down her back as she craned her neck to the sky and brought up what I had been thinking about, "Stars are beautiful tonight."

"They sure are, especially in your eyes," looking with dilated pupils, I saw the galaxies collide. She leaned up for a kiss, I smothered her with one. Sloppy drunk and high as I was, it was understandable. Dropping our cigarettes and squishing them like spiders, we went back inside.

Delilah obviously had a little cocaine while we were gone, she started talking a mile a minute, Maybelline giggled. "Damon." He slicked his hair back with his left hand, drink in his right, sipping, placing it on the table as I went back to my previous position to face him.

"Mr. Shine, how do you do?" Knowing damn well what was going on. He tapped his nose as if it were a key symbol every high-class addict knew.

"Dandy, you mind if May inhales some?" Tense at the shoulders, waiting for his response so I could ease the muscles, Maybelline would never let it down if I had some fun and she was skipped.

Showing teeth, he looked over at his wife, then back at me, busted a gut and said, "That depends, you have the next 8-ball?"

Not knowing the lingo, I was sure he did not mean the final shot in a game of billiards, my expression suggested that he should elaborate. Damon had his left hand up and covering one side of his face to help muffle the sound from any passersby, "Three and a half grams of coke."

"After the first payday?" I too looked over to the patrons near and walking by, paranoia comes as a side effect with the drug apparently.

May and Delilah watched attentively.

We shook on it like fiends.

"Was out back clear?" Damon had a paranoiac look I did not catch before.

"Yes," May chimed in.

The four of us headed out back, Damon gave me my second bump. "Wow, eyelids won't shut anytime soon after that," I said while revealing the whites at the back of my eyes.

Maybelline took her first hit with pride, wide eyed, watering like it were hot sauce instead of cocaine. "Smells like nail polish," she said, and we all slapped our knees out of breath.

"More like paint thinner," Delilah added with glee.

Wiping my nose and rubbing my gums the way Damon showed me, I agreed with Delilah, "I think you might be right. Damon, what does the scent compare to for you?"

"Heaven, bliss." I swear his eyes crossed as he said it.

Cocaine was a rush, the second time was better than the first. If we were required to run a marathon, I felt as if I would win without a doubt. We headed back into the drinking hole, slammed back another two drinks within an hour, delirious and chilled, Maybelline and I stumbled back to our apartment.

"A hell of a night" was all I had to say to her. I was to be married to the love of my life soon, start a new job Monday, and cocaine, coke was an ally. Addictive personality, was I born with it? No, I picked it up after birth to cope with tragedy. Not as a viable excuse, but I did start drinking heavily after my brother died, an intemperance as my mother tells me.

With the death of Abe and Josiah, I drank until I tripped over my own two feet. May joined me in all my proclivities, as influences went—I was bad. If you thought Jack Kerouac was a drunkard, we could have been twins in that aspect, where he was loud and obnoxious on stage—funny, but obnoxious—I was taciturn, straight to your face, and blunt.

Laying in bed that night, I stared at the ceiling like many times before, shapes, faces, ghosts haunted me. Why was I subjected to this? I do not know. My mind raced like a horse on the track, with a week's pay bet on it. The window, I always find myself looking out of a window in bed where my mind without challenge played tricks on me. What might linger out in the dark of night might be worse than what fluttered like the wings of a dove vividly in my mind. Inquisitive, I was invariably inquisitive, curious at all hours, even now. Shutting my eyes, I rolled over to comfort myself with Maybelline's embrace, she was out cold, bound to be hungover for the next day. Kissing her on the cheek settled my mind, let me fall deep, deep into slumber where the world was perfect, balanced.

Until nightmares came into the equation.

10

Weeks passed, work was smooth, easy, they say a salesman does not contain a heart. I'd say that was wrong. I took the customers' hearts, in return for a title and a brand spanking new ride with two keys and a spare tire in the rear. People came to the dealership for a reason, they knew what they wanted before I even sold them my pitch, a fastball that you wouldn't see coming. Some tried to dodge, I hardly missed a target.

A clientele sheet filled three pages after I took the two Randy had, I was an affable fellow, directly to the point and patrons preferred that. Damon was not wrong to bring me on to the team, making me "part of the family" as he called it. Selling at least a car a day, five to six days a week, depending on whether I wanted to be home all day Saturday or not. To stretch my brain, I typically did take Saturday off so I could read, drink, and smoke at leisure.

At work, we snorted lines off the tailgate of an old dilapidated Model A truck, out of sight in the back of our lot behind our repair shop, owner wrecked it a couple weeks ere I started working fingers-to-the-bone to feed my bank account with righteous dollar bills. The truck had a Coleman cooler, with a bottle cap remover made of cast iron on the side, we stashed it on the floorboard most days of the week, would fill it with Schlitz and whiskey, the seldom five dollar kind I could hardly afford before I started working there.

The guys were great, different, but aren't we all. Personal favorite of the bunch is a guy known as 'Billy The Kid', who sold vehicles with us and hung around at the old Model A on break. He was a real hoot, as my soon-to-be wife would say, his namesake came from the account that he was packing a gun seven days a week, 365 days a year and could hit a bottle at forty yards with a revolver with ease from what Damon told me. And, his real name was William, we called him Billy though for short, naturally.

Police would frown at me for what I had done, not the cocaine or drinking heavily and driving, no, buying a gun under the table with a scratched off serial number. A decommissioned World War 1 pistol was brought back by Billy's father. His dad apparently slept with it, Bill picked up the habit from his old man, evidently. Billy The Kid parted without shilly-shallying for an 8-ball of cocaine, decent handgun too. Beretta model 1915, came with a leather holster, wood grips with hash marks, iron sights, and an extra magazine loaded to the tits.

Frequently I would practice up Meadow Lake outside of Carlton, my dad would drive me, the mountain was far enough away I had to worry little about disturbing the peace. With next to nil practice, I was a hell of a shot. Some nights I would take Billy up in the hills with my dad. We shot, drank, cursed, smoked cigars, and laughed for all it was worth.

Dad enjoyed gambling, he could shoot a pistol better than me, but he did not live by it the way Billy had—when you eat, sleep, and dream something, you tend to grow to be formidable as The Kid—both would compete at a shootout, glass bottles from twenty yards, loser bought the winner a bottle of hooch, and a pack of smokes. Billy ended up receiving smokes and drink, dad just lost his temper.

After I paid Damon back with the cocaine we shook on, we shared the whole lot of it in a day's time. It was payday, and I decided to go down Third Street to a clip joint where the women were naked and the drinks were on ice. The joint's luminescent sign read: **Bleating Heart**. Damon was married, but had a hankering for women regardless of his marital ties. May and I were soon to be hitched, she did not mind that I went out with Damon as long as I did not touch. Fair enough, Damon on the other hand practically gave every lassie a suggestive look that indicated his eyes were doing more than just looking.

Trying not to shed too many bills on the strippers, I went over to the bar for drinks, two shots down the hatch and an old-fashioned in the mix, I bobbed my head to the music. Green lights shuttered, having snorted more cocaine than ever in a night, drank a whole bottle of port prior to coming here, I tripped and tripped hard.

Damon thought I choked on my vomit, overdosed or worse, had a heart attack. When he found me with my face smacked against the granite counter the barkeep was serving drinks on. "Aye!" he yelled over the noisy club, "you alive?" Smacking me on my spinal cord, "Hank!"

"What! Goddammit!" Damon, the pal he was, tilted my head back, grabbed me under his arm and walked me over to a booth, I was a mess, stable nonetheless.

Sitting my ass down like a ton of bricks, he said, "You know how to party."

Bet your ass I do, I'm proficient.

Drunk and slobbering as I spoke, "I've been known as a practitioner of the art." When you partied the way I do, it becomes an art form.

"You want to bust out of here?"

"In a little, you tired of staring at behinds and sucking on titties already?" Wiping my face, I put a cigarette to my lips, puckered and held on for dear life. The smoke billowed in my path of sight to Damon, like waves, illuminated by the flash of lights. I could have really gone for lying like a dead dog on my back down where people stepped.

Patted on the cheek to refocus my attention, "No, broad took a twenty when I meant to give her a single," aggravated, he slammed the table with balled fists, "that was worth dancing for for the whole night and then some." His "and then some" eerily sounded like a euphamism for "prostitution."

Shaking my head to show him I cared, I didn't, but I tried, he took my pack of smokes from the center of the table, tapped it against his palm once, a single cig protruded from the rest. He picked it up with his lips and lit it off the flickering candle on the table.

"This place, the name makes it sound desperate, the strippers are too." Lightheaded and leaning over on my elbows, Damon was flicking ash on the carpet, this place deserved it, where the tavern in Carlton was actually a reputable place.

"Desperate, I know, being married doesn't include your wife lusting to suffice your urges every night." He shook his head while he spoke the truth, inhaled smoke till his face went blue, blew through each of his nostrils and blinked for a moment, grabbed his vile and put a dash of cocaine on the back of his thumb. "You want any?"

Nodding, he shared a little, I was desperate too. Railing it, I said, "So, I have a proposition to make."

"What will that be?" Damon's eyes teasing as he rubbed gums 'til they bled, savoring every grain.

"See, well, you drove here right?" Before we went out tonight, I knew what was on my hidden agenda. You'd catch me driving angles every so often, recently they had all been with Damon.

"Right ... and?" Head tilted to a side, uncertain where this was going. "I did not."

He looked at me like that was obvious. "And?"

This was like walking a dog, making a sale that is: I was selling him to sell me.

"I'd like to buy one." His hands were pressed against the table as he leaned forward, closer, biting onto the hook for all it was worth.

"A car?" Eyes wide as saucers.

"Precisely. I want the three-window coupe, black and chrome." He nodded, "one out front." Now I put my hands laced together on the table, chewing on the butt of my cigarette like Red Man. The white powder was kicking in, I felt alive again, if just for a short while.

"I know which one you're talking about: the jaw dropper with black interior. Slick ride," coincidentally, he slicked his hair back while saying that.

"How about a deal?" I had something in mind, the car was already mine as far as I was concerned, he just didn't know it yet.

"Sure, shoot."

I did, "You get the bonus from the deal and take care of the paper-work that way you get your cut," he grinned like a shark approaching dinner, "but I want a hundred dollars off, and a quarter pound."

Head tilted to the side, one eye scrunched up, he looked at me be-mused, "Quarter pound of what?" Red hair cascading his face again.

"Cocaine." I sipped my drink down to the dregs, dropped the ember in an ashtray and flicked the butt at a hooker who tried to put her arm on my back.

"That's a lot of product, the hundred you will get as an employee dis-count. Far as the cocaine. I'd have to buy it, my bonus for the sale would cover that, fine. I get half." The air lifted, I had a new car coming my way and some cocaine in time for the wedding.

"Deal," he spit in his hand and I in mine, we clasped, bobbed them up and down with sinister expressions.

We went home, back to our ladies. A night on the town was nice, Damon is not as egregious as I made him out to be, sharing the cocaine helped. For a salesman, he was reasonable, most Thursdays he would make the coffee at the office for me, he said as long as the sales were good, it was his pleasure. I could sell, the money I stashed aside after a month working at the Ford dealership covered my new car, that was how well I did with sales and bonus.

11

Tuesday, after the clip joint, I had a wad of cocaine, a new vehicle fresh off the lot, a handgun at my waist, a bottle of ten-dollar whiskey under the seat to celebrate, and I was on my way back home to stun Maybelline. My dad would not have to pick me up and take me to work anymore, it was nice of him, but I felt like an inconvenience. He would just brush it off, take a short sobriety twice a day to drive me, sweet of him.

The freedom a car brought was worth the money, I had the windows rolled down and the engine working overtime, pedal-to-the-metal, speedometer read seventy-five. Although my hair was crew cut, the sensation of wind blowing through it felt ethereal, my ears rang from all the noise. I lit a cigarette and took the back way into Carlton passing the slaughterhouse.

Cops would be hard-pressed to catch me in the coupe, I did start watching my speed as I entered the town. The local police department here knew me by name, figures after you kill a man and lose two friends from gunshot wounds. Carlton's deputy was okay, he did his job, maybe adequately, depends on perspective. Far as the child-labeled chief went, the words that come to mind would have me banished from a courtroom before I finished. He was a son of a bitch, cold and to the truth, if he pulled me over with cocaine, a handgun in my possession and lacking proper identification, I'd have to kill him and skip town or serve a sentence I didn't intend on serving.

Police were not as strict back then, cocaine would get you busted sure, drinking and driving would either get you a ride home from the cop if you were too inebriated or he would let you drive off into the sunset. As far as an unmarked gun, questionable is about all that comes to mind, I know not of anyone who has had the misfortune to get busted for such a crime, but if they had, I could see serious jail time in their future. The DMV was on my to do list, hot off the lot and impatient to ride my new stallion. I decided to put off the trip for paperwork and take a test for my license. A bus was about as close to transportation besides my parents giving me a ride, I just had not had any inclination to purchase a vehicle. Scoring the job at Ford made it a hassle to get to work. Cars are a big investment, worth it however, but pricey, particularly a coupe such as mine with all the bells and whistles.

Heart skipping a beat, I saw a cop car at the side of the bridge as I entered, the lake could be seen from a mile away. I drove on, cautiously and unsuspectingly.

Honking the horn for the first time, I waited behind the wheel, bottle of whiskey in hand. May came out, curious who the stranger was in a sleek black and chrome coupe. She walked over as I honked again eagerly. "Sorry I was late, darling, I know our dinner reservations are at 8:30."

Earlier, I took my new car around for a joyride with Damon, we put a little coke on the dash and went to town on it. Having enough powder to last a month if I conserved it, this time though I went bonkers, after three lines back to back, we raced around the outskirts of McMinnville, blowing through stop signs, reckless, high, and, in a way, I felt free. Like the first time I tried the white drug. Drugs control you if you let them, they take from you, attention, money, spirit, and more than one could ever know. If you decide to do them, one day you will learn the price, or die before that day ever comes.

A man who has never drank, gotten drunk, has never lived. The alteration of mind to view light from a different orientation allows one to see both sides of a spectrum. Drugs, that is difficult to say, one might have a chance to learn more in depth who they are, one may lose their mind, overdose, or subsequently lose their mind. The outcomes are limitless, it changes you. Dabble a little too long and you get a little too far gone, pulling oneself back can be a battle to the bitter end. It's all about choosing your poison, there is no cure for the inevitable; death, life, we are all living, dying. Depending on how you see it, we are living to die, or in my case dying to live.

"Hank, … oh … my … god. Don't tell me you stole that?" She worked at the bank, but she had not been allowed to deposit my money on the clock since we were a couple. Keeping a few secrets, if it is for a good reason such as this to startle her with a new ride, did not bother me one bit.

Smirking, one side of my mouth raised, I lit another smoke and exhaled.

"Hank?" She came over to the driver side door, leaned against the window seal and gave me a dirty look I'd expect from someone whose lunch I had stolen.

"What? You said don't tell you if I stole it." She punched my arm twice, I caught her hand the third.

"No … No … You did, didn't you?" That hurt, she thought I actually had.

"Maybelline, go grab two glasses, and no … I bought it." The wry smile and a wink did not keep me out of the doghouse tonight for having my fun with her over the whole ordeal. "Fill you in on the ride."

Squinting, puzzled as I would be in her situation, she ran back inside, popped her head out the door to yell, "Let me change really fast!"

Right, fast, might as well start drinking now.

Fifteen minutes later she came out with a red bandana covering most of her raven black hair, red heels, a black satin dress that went two inches past her knees and had a provocative slit on the right that went halfway up her thigh.

"You're jaw dropping, can you hold mine up for me or should you change?"

She sat in the passenger seat blushing, laughed and pushed me flirtatiously. "Stop, you're handsome yourself, you know there, Slick."

I winked, grabbed her a cigarette and took both of the glasses, draining a dollar's worth of whiskey in each. "Tell me what you think."

"Outstanding," she rubbed red lipstick with her middle finger nail, "how much?"

"For the car or the whiskey?"

"Both." Looking up to the heavens, I put the coupe into drive, and sped down the street.

"Ten for the whiskey, and the car, matter of perspective."

She raised an eyebrow. "How so? And ten-dollar whiskey, not bad at all–fancy."

I pulled out a small bag that said "sugar" in red bold letters. "That's how," I responded to her question.

"Sugar? How does that have anything to do–" by now May, saw my pupils, the white on my nose, "oh ... oh, lord." Cocaine was a good distraction from her finding out the actual price I paid for the coupe.

"Want some, sweetheart?" For being high, I was mellowed out by the gradual shifting of gears and hum of the engine, raising pistons and releasing exhaust out of the pipe.

"Please," I could tell she was ravenous for a little, "hand the sugar here, Mr. Shine." She batted her eyes at me.

Tossing her a dollar to use as a straw and handing the sugar bag over, I watched her take almost as much as I did in one line off a book that had been on the floor. Perks of having your own vehicle, I can kick my feet up on lunch and read. And a hardcover serves as a good surface for ingesting cocaine off of.

"So, you did not rack up any debt, did you?" She lifted the bag and moved her rump to and fro, as if to settle the springs beneath black leather.

"Nope, me and Damon worked it out, this coupe was the front car in the lawn for display. After a month with a bonus and as well as I was doing with sales–one to two cars a day, on occasion, more–the car is paid for. And since I chose Damon to handle the paperwork and take the sale, we split his earnings on a quarter pound of," I shook the bag in my hand now for illustration.

"Terrific, wonder what the look on your daddy's face is going to be? You know he is a fan of coupes."

I shrugged, "Plausibly, piss his pants and drive it at the same time when I chuck him the keys."

"Take it you did not go get your license yet?" Girlfriends, fiances, even your mother, women, by and large, look out for men more than they care to admit. Hell, I'd have more things falling apart around me if it were not for May, haphazard as my life is without her to organize it.

"Not yet, need to. The hell with it though, when I get a chance I will go by the DMV and take the test."

"Ha, you think too much, Hank." Her dimples, visible as she watched me work the steering wheel for a turn. "That whiskey was great by the way, care to pour me another?"

"Hold the wheel." We were heading to Portland where our reservations were held for 8:30 p.m. sharp at an Italian restaurant Maybelline was introduced to by her parents growing up.

Hawthorn Street was packed. May held my hand until we made it to the front of Giovanni's, where I opened the door and let her in. We sat near the kitchen, my back was against the wall, paranoia can save your life.

I ordered something with meatballs and sauce, I think it came with noodles. May, she ordered a meal I did not bother trying to learn the pronunciation of, which cost more than what I spent on food in a week. Bleating Heart down Third Street in McMinnville was a clip-joint, here, this was right on par. Price-gouging, meatball-selling, son of a sniveling cur.

"Hey, I was thinking—" a waitress brought our cocktails, "thanks, here." I handed the lady a dollar and she winked at me, May kicked my shin. "Ow, I was thinking … our honeymoon—"

"What about it?" her hand grabbing my lighter off the table to get the tobacco of her cigarette burning.

"You know how you love the beach?" She was obsessed with the beach as much as I was with looking at the stars.

"Yes, oh, please tell me," Maybelline said impatiently.

"I was thinking we should go there, Pacific City?" I came forth with the idea, the specific beach was not an issue, just throwing out the one we preferred to go and visit for the day, usually when my parents or hers would drive us. Now though, with a car and everything, free rein, opportunities, adventure was in our future.

"Pacific would be the place, the waves crash against Haystack Rock and we can watch from the precipice that overlooks." The precipice that overlooks was a glorified name for BJ Rock, at least that was what me and my older brother used to call it when we went there as kids. The name came from a certain experience that involved two adolescents stumbling upon a couple; a girl with hair flailing in the wind, and the male was laying on his back with trousers down.

The name speaks for itself.

"I look forward to it." Looking into her eyes, I leaned across the table, kissed her, my legs shaky by the time I retreated–hard to handle myself when her lips were against mine.

Our meals were brought out, served off of a big tray a waitress carried on one shoulder comfortably. Let's just say the tray was deceiving for how small the plates were that were dropped off, less than what I expected and I was not expecting a whole hell of a lot. A pricey menu like the one Giovanni's had told you right there–more money, less food.

Shortly, we wrapped up at the Italian joint after three drinks apiece, a meal nothing bigger than an appetizer, and a few laughs. Maybelline was content with the food, passive I was, but whether it tasted better than what you get at the grocery store, I don't know.

We ambled out, happy to get back to the coupe and race back home. May wanted to drive, I let her after she complained that I was not sharing. For never driving before, high, and intoxicated, she did fine. We made it back home, shut the lights off and played underneath the sheets to our hearts' content.

That was just another night of my life I will never forget.

12

Mom and dad were tying cans with white woven string to the back of my coupe earlier that day, Maybelline wanted it done, even though I did not. A compromise was made: we did not paint the windows. She said I was grumpy, and I told her "no, the car, it's my baby." A day such as your wedding day already has your heart beating out of your chest, I found that out.

With an attempt to calm my nerves, I licked my finger, stuck it in my sugar bag, took a finger to my gums and brushed them until the anxiety went away. And that was prior to my mentioning of the coupe and how it was my baby, if I ever had one.

May said, "Hank, you will have a real baby."

Nodding, casually I said, "Yeah one day, never know."

"That day is today," her tone solemn, "I'm pregnant, Hank, you are going to be a father." Whether that was perfect timing or not on our wedding day, I had no idea, starstruck and mumbling to myself as if I escaped the insane asylum earlier that day.

"You ... you're joking right?" She was wearing a dress, not her wedding dress, not until later.

"Hank Shine!" May stomped her feet in contempt, I wished I were a turtle and could've slid back in my shell.

"Maybelline," I gulped, "are you definitive, you know for certain?"

"Yes, the doctor said."

I was about to bite back my words or wish I had, "You mean you went and had tests done without my knowledge?" I asked incredulously.

"Just as you went and bought a car and a bag of cocaine." Now she was starting to get irritated and I figured calming her down would be in my best interest if I desired to keep my head attached to my shoulders.

"Honey, that is terrific news–fantastic! I'm just, I'm shocked … today is a surreal day, marriage and all. And a kid, we are going to have our own–"

"It's too early to tell whether it is going to be a boy or girl yet."

"Regardless, we are fortuitous enough to have this change our lives, May, it will be the start of a family of our own." Optimistic, I had my head in the clouds, but who was to tell me that was a bad idea. Father, me? That was a thought before, planning it out never came about, now it was really happening.

"Yes, oh, I am so glad you're okay with it." Her face, that of delight, relaxing at my words.

"This is spectacular." I grasped her around the waist and planted one on her lips, she lifted one leg up, I spun her in a circle and made sure my dance moves were not rusty.

In the street at my parents' place, dancing to no music at all, mom and dad thought we were madly in love, we were, but that was not why we were dancing. When I mentioned it to my mom, she lifted herself up out of the depressing state she had been in for the last five or six years since my brother passed. Dad said he was going to cut back on the drinking, but he never did.

13

Inviting family, friends, and whoever else, can be a veritable pain in the ass. Organizing your wedding takes a lot of patience and commitment. It all came through eventually, we did not have a big turnout, twenty–thirty people max. Our location was a fenced off acre–my parents backyard, it was free and spacious. Chairs were lined up, people came with bottles of alcohol, Damon brought Cuban powder, which I helped myself to liberally before, in the middle, and post. Delilah had her hair done up nice with her parents there at her side, Billy The Kid stopped by, offered to be my personal bodyguard, I declined after thanking him.

As Maybelline's father walked her down the aisle, I told myself yet again how lucky I was. She was ravishing, drop-dead gorgeous, black hair complimenting her dress, I did not know why I was so fortunate, she made life worth living. Saying our vows, we kissed for minutes, the spectators cheered us on, drunk off love, intoxicated from twenty-dollar whiskey, those minutes rolled by faster than you'd think.

A moment I would not mind living over again and again.

The music played well past 3:00 a.m., cops came by, informing us the neighbor put in a noise complaint–multiple times. Inviting the cops in for a free beer and a shot of high-quality hooch, they walked in and stayed for awhile. I had the first dance with the beautiful bride, our peers whistled and clapped, knowing damn well we had practiced. Having the time of our lives, kissed with wet lips, smoked tobacco, I was on my second pack within three hours.

Damon made a toast, wished us the best and thanked me for entering his life. Delilah, she nearly fell over on her face in vomit by the time she was going to give a toast, her husband ran her into my parents' house to wash off and head home. May made an announcement to everyone about her pregnancy, five months or more and we would have our own tyke running around with Maybelline's face and my eyes or vice versa.

Who the hell knows, I was new at this.

Belligerently drunk, I was happy, I did not forget a single moment, and, if I did, how was I supposed to know? Escorted by the cops back home, I took back any insults I had ever uttered about them, just this once. May got the door, I sounded like a stampede of elephants running through the house, I ran in joy, arms raised like a plane, swerving, flying. Maybelline swiftly followed after me, shaking her head. We danced to a record in the living room, did cocaine off the kitchen counter, it was 5:00 a.m. before we knew it, and the sun was cresting the horizon.

Dangerous as it was, reckless, plain stupid, but worth it–leaning a ladder against the apartment, we climbed with intoxicated movements and got to the roof in one piece, sat where there was not a patch of moss to dampen our hinds, May rested in my arms while the sun blinded me. Just when I thought our celebration was over, we dashed back inside, stripping our outfits off all the way to our bedroom, Mr. and Mrs. Shine making love like it was the first time.

Our wedding day.

14

Honeymoon, the history behind the term is intriguing. With the money we had received from our wedding, we bought the nicest room we could rent for the weekend, life was moving up. I parked the coupe down below on a weather warped-street, out front where I could watch it. Car thieves run rampant when tampering is only a twist of a screwdriver or bash of the window with an elbow wrapped in cloth.

When we were in our suite, shortly we could be caught by paparazzi if fame were in our fortune as we overlooked the beach from a balcony high above, top floor, five-star, and drinking brandy on the rocks, bag of corn chips on the table, salsa, bean dip, Mexican entree. Gusts of wind spit sand at my face like hail, in my eyes, and tasting it was like rocks grinding at my teeth, for that I was less than pleased.

"The waves, what do you see?" Drunk, May asked her arms swaying as much as the kite overhead, twenty feet above the hotel, a kid running hither and thither trying to tame a flying object gone over the edge, radical, wild, out of control. His ball cap to the side, pack of gum in his shirt pocket till it fell out, along with baseball cards, and round polished marbles.

"Water splashing, moving?" Not sure of the answer she was searching for, I pinched my eyelids as sand pestered my eyes. I sneezed, she patted my back, coughing, wheezing, knocked the tray full of ash off the table, sun boring down, face felt green, man I am sick, sick of this goddamn sand.

"No, what do you feel as you see the water splashing and moving, Hank?" May picked up the ashtray, took a size seven ladies shoe to sweep the debris into the roaring air without a care, littering, punishment, not that we knew. Who was watching, keeping track, cops, deputy, there were none, this vacation was surely in store for fun.

The sun was bright overhead, focusing all of its attention on white as a ghost skin, it burnt, man did it burn, seventy-five degrees out and windy. I had shorts, sandals and a sleeveless shirt on, plaid, not bad, lighting my last smoke, deep in thought, pondered her question. Smoke rolled out of my nose the same way it had with Damon before when I watched him mulling over a deal where I spit the spiel, a habit I was soon to pick up.

"Well, I see water, blue, shaky, calm in the distance, up where the children slide on skimboards, it's receding only to come back and crash down again. Motions transfixing like an illusion from a crackerbox magician, soothing like honey, kitsch, laughable, takes your mind away and relaxes. I don't know what I am trying to say, the ideas faint and far away, far as being a poet goes, I need practice."

Reaching for a brown-tinted bottle next to my chair, tipping legs off the ground, I felt the liquid doing its job. "Here, Mrs. Shine," I said with a Kentucky accent, "mead, fits the moment, honeymoon and all." She received a crooked grin from me, followed off by a belly full of laughter.

"Mead is worth the agonizing hangover,"–true, drink the beverage and face the repercussions later–she sipped and wiped her lips, "definitely."

"Right you are, the taste rivals domestic beer, gets you drunk quick too." Took a drag from my smoke till my lungs were full and ready to quit, like a good husband, I handed it to May, she took a few drags herself before passing it back, chill and relaxed.

"So, May," she looked at me with awkward eyes, losing herself in my pupils every bit as dark blue as the ocean, far out where daring men dive, "what do you see as you look at the waves?"

Her hair was tucked behind pointy ears, suntan lotion applied to the tip of her precious button nose, a yellow dress with shoulder straps revealing her chest, hiding round succulent breasts, showing enough, but not too much, to make me wary of men drifting by. She is my wife, my love, God could not split us from his kingdom above.

"I see my mom and dad running with hair splashed by wind, as if age did not take that from them." Her parents were not in the best of health, nor mine. Drinking and smoking and partying at jazz clubs that were open till 4:00 in the morning will do that to you after an extended period of time. But the promise of a child and being grandparents gave them hope. Hope, when lost, ages a man, when returned, it's like a spell counting back the minutes on the clock.

"They're chasing me, knocking over sandcastles, picking me up and putting me on their shoulders, taking turns," a subtle tear, small, but there, was brought to her eye, "there's more, with the tide I see peace, tranquility," her gaze focused on the ocean, we were a half mile away and had the best view in the house, "captivating, Hank, as your eyes when I fall deeply within." At this moment I leaned over the minute table, nearly flipping it with my weight until her arms balanced it out as I kissed her, salty lips, luscious, and soft as plush toys untouched by kids, the taste of cheap beer and expensive liquor, cigarettes, and Mexican appetizers. Our noses bumped, rubbed back and forth, we paused until later when we would be huddled in our room.

"Right you are, the ocean is pretty, but not as pretty as the ocean in my eyes and all the secrets, notions, and lust whirlpooling around, sucking you in for due time." She giggled, grabbed my arm with small pale white lotion-used hands to stand me up, jazz played in the background, saxophones and trumpets blaring upbeat, the beat at the moment moved your feet, woke up those who tried to sleep, horns, drums keeping a steady fast rhythm.

I put my hand to the small of her back and guided her movement, feet stepped in sync, the tap of heels, clasp of hands, sway of hips, we were so in love, it was visual. Ascending her right hand, I spun, once, twice, three times. Smoke getting in my eyes, as viewing all that hit me, wife, romance, at the beach, mine, mine, mine. A future, a future for me, my brother up above staring down at me now, parting the fluffy clouds, wafting away incoming thunderclouds, rain ceasing, joy, joy, joy.

"Let's go walk down to the beach, grab your classy bottle of wine, my dear." May stepped first back out of the dance quarter, I went for the glasses and she for the wine, looked for snacks in case we got hungry and wanted to dine.

"Grab my smokes, will you, love." My expression looked as if I were high, I was, not oblivious, but close, enjoying a good old time.

"Are they in your purse?" I asked politely, unsure, I had my lighter from the days at the track, but frankly that was it.

"Yeah, front pocket, matches too." How did I know, smokes get lost in her purse like dollar bills at the clothing outlet in Portland, where she shops for dresses, garments, slacks, shoes with heels—and money I can't afford to spend on that.

"Brought my lighter, no need." Striking matches would be futile, the happenstance of that working is next to nil unless we were to barricade the wind. "Oh, here, found them." Who knew how long it would be until we were back cozy in our room, plenty of smokes and alcohol was a prerequisite to having a grand time in our minds, and last, but not least, cocaine. A hit here and there kept a man sane, for me at least.

Slamming the door shut, loud and echoing, just like our bastard neighbor back home. Bad habits are picked up without your knowledge at times, see an individual do it once, no big deal, twice, thrice, you join in, split, attached, spliced. May skipped down the red carpeted stairs, she looked like a sunflower with that yellow dress as she moved quicker than my eyes could follow, beauty, true beauty, I gulped and swallowed.

In truth, the ocean, as vast and gorgeous as it is, makes me woozy, the ambiance is surreal, I just had to make sure that my seasickness did not affect our night and mess with how I felt. 7:00 p.m. is what my seven dollar watch strapped to my wrist told, scuffed and battered by years of brushing against objects, inadvertently. The sun stood high in the sky earlier when drinks were first poured, now it was going down over the ocean as the sand got closer, knocking right at our door.

May stepped up the four-inch construction yellow painted curb, trotting through a white-striped, fading dusty parking lot with a basket in hand and a bottle of vintage red wine from Paris. A magnificent sight stuck out like a sore thumb, Haystack Rock was stupendous as the first time we crossed paths back when I was six or eight and my brother ran me down to the oceanfront to share its beauty with me. I'd imagine it could be seen from the moon, if ever did I become an astronaut–which I highly doubted, given my drinking and drug use–that would be the number one thing I would test out.

My sandals were taken off and inserted in a plastic bag and shoved in the basket along with Maybelline's. I grabbed it from her, I wouldn't allow a lady to carry all of that weight. Chivalry isn't dead, not if you find a darling you want to stick with until the end and nightly take her to bed.

"Would you like to head up the side there?" I asked with gesticulating hands. She looked over to our right, a mountain of sand and to the left led out to BJ Rock.

"Grab me a cigarette and light it, will you, darling?" I said showing teeth, a fiend for a nicotine rush.

"Very much so, we can sit at the precipice and watch the sun go down, you can see for miles out into the wicked waves as they creep and ebb." May put a cigarette in my mouth, kissed me on the cheek, where rosy red lipstick marked me hers, grabbed my lighter out of my denim back pocket and scored the flint until a flame precariously played with the wind. The first time was a failure, the wind snatched the flame, second was taken by a sly gust intolerable for fire, by the third time, trying to keep the fire burning, she lost it.

"Here, just put your hand where it will block the fire from the wind– cup it, sweetheart." She did as I had instructed, a second later I was taking a drag, my head felt like a balloon primed to catch a trip on a one-way to the promised land.

Wading through tan sand, soft, dry like a salted slug, and warm from the heat, my unconditioned legs ached from labor, my buzz was fading, it took us fifteen minutes to reach the base of the hill. Going from sand to rock like broken glass, I cursed as pieces jabbed heel and between tender toes, too lazy to put my shoes back on. May went wild, dancing through the minefield as if it were nothing more than a walk in the park. I bit back the urge to tell her to stop making me look like a damn fool over here swearing at trivial matters as she ran freely. She deserved her fun when she could get it, working at the bank was a stressful job. Most days of the week she went straight for the bottle, no glass, just drinks from the bottle.

Customers will do that to you.

Approaching a miniature jungle with vines and grass that could cut you like paper, sand was below however, and not rock, to my relief. A gradual declivity made of rigid terrain and washed out rock, we passed through the next obstacle, after a trek we were at the precipice May was so eager to reach. Water rippled, wakes kicked ten feet high behind a boat the size of the Titanic, a large cruise ship had people leaning against metal railing while staring at the stupendousness of Haystack Rock, much as I was at that moment. Elevation at par with the top of Haystack, in the distance happy, playful whales kicked tails out into the sunset, smacking down to splash water for hundreds of feet around. A sight most have in their dreams, and we, we are here living it like there is no tomorrow.

I felt so good I could die.

"Would you like to sit down, Maybelline?" She was busy gazing, fathoming what a tremendously lavish sight this was. Seagulls chirped and whistled, hissed for food, soared, cut through the wind to scoop fish a hundred feet below our position.

"Yes, very much so." I grabbed a plain white towel from her shoulder and spread it where we could sit.

I had just finished laying it out, when May requested, "Move it closer, Hank, I want to sit on the edge."

"Daredevil, aye, okay, let's do it." Moving the towel close enough to the edge where we were able to dangle feet off, perched here made me feel like I was skydiving, heart throbbing as if I skipped out on death. May plopped down hard, she had drank too much, same as I. Placing the basket to my left, I pulled out the bottle of wine and popped the top with some effort and a pair of keys, corks and fancy drink as this was not my style by any means.

"We don't need the glasses, I'm not afraid of catching any germs from you," she said to me as I started to pull the wine glasses out. Don't get me wrong, once in a while drinking straight from the bottle was acceptable. No one else was out that I could see, the wind was chilly, but we were warmed by the red as blood alcohol that soon saturated my innards.

"What a relief, in that case." Taking a gulp, I passed it to her, wine was alright, not great but alright.

"That's really good, actually," May mentioned, as if shocked.

"You're trying to tell me you purchased that without knowing whether it was good or not?" I was incredulous, money was money, but thirty dollars for red wine from Paris seemed like an utter waste. Cheap, expensive, all tastes like dyed piss, colored with choosing of food coloring and sold for a price the bum down the street could work his whole life for and never afford.

"Well, I heard from a friend who heard from a friend–"

I cut her off there. "Who heard from their friend, I get it, you gambled, this hand you won." I gave her a wicked grin. "Next time, thirty dollars could have bought us enough to get drunk on for a month." Which was absolutely true, I could drink twenty-cent bottles of vodka all week long, throw in some orange juice and voilà–screwdrivers, which are a pleasure I indulge in quite frequently. Cheap can be good, mix it with a soft drink, coffee and honey, juice, even a shake, and you get white-trash drunk off of twenty-cent vodka. Can't beat that.

Gravely, May put it to me, "Don't interrupt me,"–as if I were so rude and inconsiderate–"I was trying to say they heard it from a person who heard it from a person who worked at a vineyard. See, I was getting to it,"– not fast enough–"hold your horses once in a while, Mr. Shine." Gulping down a small fraction of the devil's blood, Maybelline passed it back.

"Here, I thought cheap whiskey put hair on your chest and dropped your balls, this stuff here is a real tongue twister," I spoke with enthusiasm, dry and uncaring.

"I'm no wine connoisseur, but I'd like to say that is the point. Fermented grapes tend to give off an eerie taste." Eerie, that's one way to put it, considering someone's feet could have mashed the grapes I was imbibing.

66

Nasty, nasty business, where do people get off smashing grapes with feet like it were some kind of pleasurable activity, then to drink it–count me out of that jazz, sounds like wine lovers have a foot fetish to me. I made an exception because it was our honeymoon, and getting drunk is getting drunk, without a drink to do it, it doesn't happen. I bore with her for the time being and squinted like I'd eaten a brick of cheese and were using the pot, I tried, attempted, drank this repugnant beverage she called wine and I called the devil's blood.

"Thought you loved wine?" Confused, she bought it, why the hell would you buy something just to buy it … women.

"Uh…" Cat had her tongue, caught her like she catches me when I absentmindedly don't share. Forgetting is fair, but I understand why she cares.

"Well, that's what you said when you were buying it." I looked at her lost, if she forked over the money for no apparent reason, I might as well have given some to the homeless man holding a sign on the corner, begging for change, peace, and prosperity.

"Clarify for me, will you, May?" Irritated, but sedate at the same time–a man of many talents, jack of all trades and master of none, I know I get it a lot from my wife–my personality was splitting and I was doing all I could to hold it at the seams. Honeymoons were a time of joy, intimacy, and various other things.

I had to keep my cool.

The drug, that was what I forgot, time passed by, a little was all I needed to straighten myself out, buff out the divots, seal the crevices, mend the demons lashing out.

"Well I, I saw the price really and … reasoned it was good," my girl said with too much naivete.

That is how I sell cars to fools, some cars are clunkers driving out of the parking lot, people treat them as if they were gold just because a whopping sign is placed that reads 3,000 dollars. I run up and give them the best pitch of my life, hock a beater for a prize at the end of the month when my bonus comes through. Too, sports cars are a pit you throw your money into in most cases, people piss away money on foreign exotic cars, they run for a hundred miles then have to be tuned like a motorcycle, fixed like a boat, "bust out another thousand for a mechanic". At least with a motorcycle, you can bring it into the comfort of your house, drink a beer, and watch TV while you fix it.

"May, I swear sometimes," I shook my head, had to mollify the severity if we were to avoid a quarrel, it was our honeymoon after all, "you crack me up, you really do, hell, whatever, let's enjoy it while it lasts." She took the bottle back from my hands and elbowed me in the ribs as I pulled her close, the air was chilly.

"This is one of my favorite spots in the world, well two, actually." May was being clever and I hadn't had to try and decipher, easy, I could read her too. When you are painstakingly around someone for years, it is hard not to pick up or not have an aptitude for reading them.

"The beach and this cliff?" Acting as if I were oblivious to allow her a shrewd moment.

She looked at me with relaxed green eyes, reflective as emeralds, shiny as dew on grass on a midsummer's morning. "No silly," bashful, but dignified, she said, "the cliff and in your arms, Hank," her voice was soft as fresh snow on the mountain, and about as sweet as any candy I've ever had.

We kissed with chapped lips, drank wine from a bottle like homeless men do on the street, disguising it with a brown paper bag, and looked over the ocean while the sun went down. I had an itching for a line really bad, so I snorted one off the back of my hand, May did as well. Inhaling cocaine was tricky with the wind threatening to blow it all away, we managed though. Being able to share a moment like this was worth anything, I'd go through anything for Maybelline. Our honeymoon was something special, a night spent at the edge of a cliff with feet dangling, where stars came twinkling out in a wide-open sky, I pointed out the Milky Way, she asked me questions for an astronomer, good thing I knew a thing or two.

15

The weekend at the beach went by fast, we dared not freeze in the water so we didn't go for a swim. Pictures were taken by a photographer who we hired for a nickel.

Five photographs were shot and produced, two with the sand dunes hulking at our backsides, two with Haystack Rock looming in the background, and the last with May in my arms as we kissed. I had her picked up, legs were tangled around my waist like a boa constrictor, and sand got in my eye metaphorically, that's what I told Maybelline anyways, crying from love is not shameful, just embarrassing when you were the only one doing so at the moment. I was glad the resolution was not sharp enough to pick up tears.

Five grainy photographs were snugly placed in the sleeve of a book I had brought along for the trip, now serving as a shield against the elements. If the old adage is correct and a picture speaks a thousand words, I am sure each word would consist of four letters: L-O-V-E. Love can be spoken in different ways throughout languages, imagery, messages, but felt best by the heart.

Dishing over the bills for a real meal, we dined at Pacific Cities beachfront restaurant, coincidentally it was renamed "Hank's Bar and Grill" since last I was there, wasn't my bar, though I did act like it were. I was treated to a hearty burger that clogged my arteries as well as the cigarettes I smoked. May drank gin and played slot machines in the back, no money was won, but that was not the point, she said, the point was to have fun and, by God, she did.

An older gentleman asked me to play a game of pool as he saw me hunched over watching Maybelline spend my spare change on the lottery, I accepted his offer. Thirty bucks were slapped down on the blue felt befitting a throne for a king, I did my own kind of gambling and won. Close is close, but when it comes down to it there is one victor and one loser, with as much dignity as I can put into words. I hate to lose and rarely ever do.

Within no time on Monday, I was back at the lot, snorting lines in the office and out back on a crashed and totaled Model A truck's tailgate, drinking what was left over of a rich man's liquor from a flask and moving with the times. Maybelline was licking her fingers, counting bills, delving out change, checking accounts, and eating the free cookies and drinking the free coffee they had available for the patrons.

Life moved on, we were married, finished a wonderful honeymoon that filled our wanderlust for a spell, and lastly, but more importantly, had a junior on the way.

16

Stressful does not even put the feeling on the map when your wife has a belly that kicks every time you whisper at it, my child has it out for me, I swear. There is something demonic laying dormant, just waiting for a chance to get out and wreak havoc–little hellion. If I was cracked out to be a father, I would find out long after deciding babies were not freaky. Kids, I loved kids, being twenty-three, people thought I was still one myself. I wouldn't argue either with the elders I worked with, typically they were right in saying I still had maturing to do. Even those elders have maturing of their own to do, hard to break as old dogs, they probably never will.

Maybelline took a maternity leave after her water broke abruptly while removing a safety deposit box from the wall in the bank's vault. All transpired on the clock, I told her to take a leave sooner, but that girl never listens when it comes between work. She was adamantly saying "I will work and that's how it will be, sitting around the house will drive me crazy." Which in all respect to those of which are stuck in the house all goddamn day long, it does, it really does.

Solitary confinement would kill me.

Wednesday afternoon, when I had received an emergency call from the hospital claiming my wife was about to give birth across town, Damon threw me my jacket and gave me a line to inhale off his desk before I ran out the door and burnt tires through third gear as I drove through back streets like a bat out of hell. It was madness, my driving record was clean, though it shouldn't have been after all of the stunts I'd pulled throughout my time behind a wheel. Man, did I have fun though, I knew what I was doing too, a second sense I picked up with nothing more than a passion for driving fast and being reckless as a one-legged junkie with nothing to live for.

When I had arrived, she was shrieking from what sounded like a sort of torture they did overseas, horrible, horrible, interrogation tactics were implemented, unspeakable things happened, the thought of history makes a man who was living through it sick to his liquor-soaked stomach. Opening the door to her room, she raucously yelled as if eaten alive, being beaten to death with a cane, or bamboo slivers were skewering her from underneath all of her nails simultaneously. Muffling my ears by use of hands to diminish the horrible noise she was projecting, I stood at her side while the spectacle was being viewed by a doc and nurse. Our parents were old, and old people know well enough, if a baby is born, might as well rest and relieve yourself from it while you still can. Far as support went, mentally and physically I was here for her, all in, my eggs were all in her basket so to speak.

I felt bad, I really did, it was a tragedy, where I only viewed it instead of participating. She screamed, tears came to her eyes throughout the whole process, giving birth was horrific and I was glad to be a man. At a later date, I would explain to her (in a jocular manner) how getting kicked in the testicles was worse on a pain scale. My reasoning was that if a male were ever kicked in his family jewels and asked if he wanted to have it done again, he would decline immediately while he dry-heaved for a half-hour. Girls, the next thing they say after squealing like a stuck pig for hours is "I want another." Insanity, if there ever were an adequate illustration.

Grateful is how I put it to her, that I made it in time to see my newborn exit womb and come into this life head first. Remarkably, a gross sight, "that's nature" our doctor said as he smacked me on the back with bloody gloves and told me I would make a great dad. I knew I was high, stressed, and disheveled, clothes ruffled and unkempt as my hair after

I tousled it. That was when the reality of being a father hit me like a freight train.

The nurse asked if I wanted to hold my son. With fear of dropping him, I cradled his small form with the utmost care. Maybelline wanted me to hold the child first, she said, after months of carrying him, it was my turn, we worked evenly as a team and I had some catching up to do. Considering I was the one able to drink and do coke for the last few months, smoke cigarettes to my heart's content while she quit cold turkey after our honeymoon, I agreed with the statement.

I will never forget the moment I held my son for the first time, tears cascading down my face like a waterfall, the exhaustion of not sleeping lately caught up with me. Currently, I was drinking more than ever to deal with my wife being pregnant, and moody as the weather in Oregon— the doc used the word bi-polar to classify. A part of me could not fathom my child actually in my arms at that moment. Happiness exuding from his presence, a little ball of delight, warm as laundry finished after a cycle in the dryer. His eyes were blue like mine, nose was May's, jawline was mine, forehead was identical to mine, ears were like mine, he took after me, predominantly.

The weight of the world was lifted off my shoulders as I looked over at Maybelline and saw that my wife was healthy, breathing, and in control. I could take a full breath finally and sigh from relief. At that moment I felt more like a man than ever, deciding to abstain from cocaine as it was a rich man's drug and I had responsibilities now more than ever. This kid needed me, and, by God, I was going to be the best dad to ever walk this earth.

Names are hard to decide–collectively. I could come up with a dozen off the top of my head if I put my mind to it. May was picky, to appease her we agreed with my second choice instead of the first, our son was named James. My first choice would've been Bernard, but May said she did not want her small fry to have a name kids would be picking on him for, calling him St. Bernard, the dog boy–I see her point. I chose it because it had a sophisticated ring to it, a man of high stature, James was fine too. Less risk of anyone calling my son a dog, less risk of me having to kick a kid's ass for bullying.

17

Time scurried by after the day my son was born. Inevitably it does, but with your first kid and those to come if you are inclined to have more, it goes faster than you might think. Before I knew it, life was already two paces ahead of me. I was just trying to consecutively tackle each new step that was brought my way or that I barged into head on. Choices needed to be made, prioritizing, I remained an honest man, decided I needed to be there for my family each and every day, and live my life to the best of my abilities. I realized that my happiness was a determinant of whether my wife or son would be happy, I had to stay positive.

Living an optimistic life is harder than one would reckon, albeit I was going to try.

Maybelline took leave from work for the first six months, she cursed and whined about having to stay at home so much, but for James, she was willing to break her back and challenge the sanity of her mind. Staying home night and day for six months could make your hair fall out if you're not wise and do not build a routine to preoccupy the capacity of your mind.

My parents house was two blocks from the bank down Kutch Street, before May went to work, James was dropped off with my mom. Mother was the prime candidate since Dad drank and smoked in his study religiously, thankfully, my mom cut back the days James was crawling around. Strange sight to see your boy playing on the same floor or in the same backyard as you had growing up. Toys I left behind in cardboard boxes taped shut and labeled "Hank Jr's Toys" were found in the attic and placed downstairs for a later date when James was big enough to play with them like I had.

We lived in a one bedroom apartment in the heart of Carlton near the pool, which was open in the summer for the kids. Children played basketball on the court with chain nets and wood backboards, a white half-court line and an old whitewashed mechanics shop with chipped wood and busted glass windows enclosed one side. Scrawny, sniveling little boys and cute, shy girls screamed over a game of tag on the old rickety play structure up long past its use, more a hazard now than anything.

Noise can add up, the constant battle with pretentious neighbors, vehicles racing by your apartment at odd hours with throaty exhaust that rattled our front door, dogs with bastard owners allowing them to yap, the city, town, frankly I had enough for now. Growing up down Kutch Street, now living over on Pine Street with James and Maybelline, it was time for a change, a move. Away from noisy neighbors and barking dogs, a back road, countryside living sounded ethereal to me.

I saved every hard-earned dime and penny, cut back my drinking reasonably enough, smoked a pack a day instead of two, and quit going out as much. I continued to bust my ass selling cars, working six days a week, instead of five, for the extra money so my family and I could afford a new life, a new location out of the central area of town. Damon was upset, but understanding, when I told him me and cocaine had to part ways for a while, if not for good. No more cocaine blues at the clip joint down the busiest street in McMinnville where Damon got his face slapped with titties and pants bunched by the firm ass of coke-dependent strippers, all for a buck. No more late nights at bars where the billiards games were free and the people who gambled lost and proclaimed me a pool shark. No more burning gas on backroads testing the limits and capability of my coupe's engine. I had to slack back on buying Cuban cigars for my dad and helping my mother out with purchasing alcohol. Disciplining myself took more will than I thought, it was arduous at first, but, with anything, time seems to ease the difficulty, if only just a bit.

Drugs are a terrible addiction. Cutting out the cocaine, I had to find who I was again. Alcohol helped numb the urge, along with tobacco, but it was so profound some evenings, I would punch the brick wall till my knuckles would bleed. Withdrawals had me edgy, sometimes out of control, my mannerisms were off and I was acting like a lunatic. I kept it all in, that was the hardest part, my wife, she did not need to see it, nor my baby boy.

Work was rough, I became furious, stress was a huge needle thrashing at my brain, co-workers frustrated me more than the customers who asked a million questions. After time, this rage I felt from the lack of cocaine in my system started to subside. Only with time, the interval in between was the hardest to be rational. A son and a wife were the two sole reasons my brains were not blown out of the back of my skull and painting the walls for all to see.

Eventually, I became stable, rational again, less of a hazard to those around me, I could sleep a full night's rest, wake up hungover or drunk the next day and start all over again. I found who I was again with the adoration of my wife, and lovable little son that reminded me of myself with every passing day.

I could do this and I would, for my family.

18

A house, our new home was purchased down Old Mac Highway on the outskirts of Carlton, where the farmers cultivated, grew wheat and grass for seed, stacked hay bales ten high during the blazing summer with a crew of ornery kids out of school for break. Further down at the dairy, heifers were raised for milk and steers slaughtered for meat. Vitners grew their grapes to smash with feet and ferment in the dark dampness of an old red barn with a steel roof rusted to a crimson tinge that leaked from heavy rains, and snow-covered winters, where the feet of powder creaked and weighted it down, and swayed with the 55 miles an hour gusts in fall.

Blue clouds with fluffy qualities drifted overhead during the months after winter, spring held a forecast for rain making for a dingy sky. The fields would turn moist and swell up with water, farmers cursed at the small lakes drowning their crops from asshole neighbors whose culverts were angled to drown out fields. The oink of pigs could be heard while passing by, the thought of bacon and eggs were always brought to mind.

Old Mac Highway, a two-lane road with no speed limit posted, covered like an acne- ridden teen, pimpled with potholes hammered into existence from log trucks, tractors, and semis racing down the road like a speedway. A divider traced the highway for a mile until it hit gravel, where leftover cherry juices coated rock and sodden dirt to fend against dust in the dryer seasons when dust became a nuisance.

To me this sounded like home.

"You know, I always loved Carlton," May said, while looking at our new house from the lawn out front, riddled with gopher holes and weeds that needed to be hacked out of existence.

"Me too, one day this town will expand and our property will be worth a large chunk of change." There were forty acres, the neighbor was willing to lease our land for a pittance and farm it, share the profit, and, on top of all of that, we were issued a tax break. Every break I could get at this point would keep James in diapers, food on the table, and drink in my hand to take the edge off from restless nights when my son whined, bawled, and beat his fists against his crib. A crib to us, but a cage to the little one.

"Right you are, Hank." She grabbed my hand, warm and reassuringly, James was in a white painted wicker stroller with the top pulled down to keep him from getting chilled. "This is a good location out here," May said as she looped the thumb of one hand in the belt loop of her green corduroy jeans.

"Remote ... huh ... no neighbors to wake us at night, our own drive-way. I can piss outside without charges being filed." She only laughed and shook her head at my jest. "Things are looking up for us, Maybelline, they really are." I squeezed her hand.

Our driveway was a quarter of a mile long with grass down the center and gravel down the sides. I knew that I would have to level the driveway out the best I could and mow the grass down the center, my coupe was bottoming out in some areas. The closest house on either side was far enough away, I did not dwell on being woken at 3:00 in the morning or cursed for drinking and playing music until 3:00 a.m., it goes both ways when you live in town. It was hard enough getting sleep with James bawling at all hours of the night, day, and morning, I was lucky to get a break at work.

Coffee extra black and no creamer, shot of whiskey, depending on the morning, and what my stomach could handle. Cigarettes were smoked and alcohol drank as a crutch to keep my eyes open as I drove the coupe to work and back after tireless days and nights.

"Single story was a good choice, Hank." May pointed out, "There is an attic if we need to store any belongings as well, hopefully no birds or spiders are nested up there." She could critique and praise all she wanted, this house was our new home and I was going to make the best of it that I could. My father taught me that, make the best with what you have and say the hell with what you don't. With everything revolving around me, standing here at this point in time was special. The first house I'd bought, where I decided to plant my roots, I couldn't believe how much life could change over a few years.

Unbelievable.

"Sure was, honey, no stairs to worry about when we grow older." I was only 25, but the future was coming fast and I did not feel like dragging my ass up and down the stairs seven days a week. "The attic will be fine, I'm sure of it, don't get in an uproar if there is a spider or two, a few starlings or even a bat up there."

"Bat, or did you say rat?"

"Well, I did not mention rats, but I am sure there might be some of those too." Her face was a few shades whiter as I laughed.

"Bats likely carry rabies, Hank, we need to make sure that James is safe, you'll have to run up there and check first thing, okay." I liked how I was automatically volunteered, rabies and all, and she put me first to receive a disease.

"Ah ... my back ... hurt it at work," bending over stretching, her glare cut straight through clothes and flesh to melt my bones and fry my marrow, "I don't know, May, you may have to climb up there. Walking around on the lot, I tweaked it, had to push Billy's truck near the coupe when his battery died last week." She started shaking her head back and forth, as if I condemned her to hell and asked her to dive out of a plane without a parachute "No way in hell," her words enunciated and cold, "you know how I feel about rats and bats, Mr. Shine, no," she squirmed from shivers running up her spine.

"We are not technically in hell ..." I shrugged my shoulder and bit a lip, while raising eyebrows the way James did when he had to defecate.

"Hank, no need to be a smartass." Her tone made it sound personal.

"Come on, I was just having some fun."

"Fun for you."

Putting a hand on her shoulder, I grabbed the flask from my blazer's inner pocket and sipped down whiskey from Dublin that was rather good. "Alright, way to spoil it. You can take care of the rats and I will deal with the bats, fair?"

"No, what the hell? How much have you been drinking, your logic's more screwed up than usual, Hank. Pass that over here." May grabbed for my flask, I held it back and waved a finger in her face.

"Ah .. Ah .. Ah. We share, remember, you make dinner tonight then and I will take care of any rodents lingering around. Just don't burn the place down, we just bought it." When she ripped the flask from my grasp, I only sneered and stuck my tongue out at her in a jocular manner.

"We will see about that," she took a nip from the flask, "biscuits and gravy, bacon, maybe your favorite fluffy pancakes the way your mom taught me how to cook. But, I am not going into that attic until it is a hundred percent, positively, absolutely, thoroughly cleaned." When your wife makes it final to that extent you just nod your head and shut up, but, me being a hell of a salesman, I could not resist to add a little more to her role.

"Breakfast for dinner, I approve. However, I want waffles too."

"Fine." I kissed her to make up for acting like a jerk.

Our new home needed tender loving care in some areas, it would have to be reshingled in the summer, painted another color besides the godawful red, trim would have to be replaced inside and out, windows resealed, gutters unclogged and nailed back into place in some areas. There was work to be done, it was our home and that was all that mattered. Something of our own, where we could grow old together and die like the people who lived here long before we purchased it from children who it was passed down to.

Apple trees, cherry, pear, and plum grew fruit out back behind the shed where wood would be stored to heat the house for cold months to come. Flowers, roses, tulips, carnations, daisies, daffodils, an array of hedges and trees grew without maintenance around the perimeter of the homestead. A shop with salmon-colored paint, bleached by the sun and nested hornets in a corner near the eve was to the left of the front door to our new house. This was going to take some time, the price was right, location was right, no spooky ghost stories spread like wildfire, it was good to go.

Three rooms inside the house, a master bedroom with two windows and a sliding door that had a lock just in case a ballsy burglar tried to break in. The second largest room was decorated with paintings of old actors, quotes from legends, clocks and maps, an old record player was left on a table with the needle placed on a dusty record where years of dust evidently accumulated. Whoever died, gave this place to their children, who decided that when they inherited this place it was not worth the time to go through and clear it out, their loss and my gain. The third room was near the entrance of the house, entering there was a moldy mattress stained yellow from orange juice or piss, probably the latter. There was a single window, and an old sewing machine with a foot pedal. This room was more a spinster's room, as I saw clothes stacked needing patches, material cut in strips and pin cushions with a thousand needles lying around.

Our new living room needed new carpet, cobwebs dusted, walls painted, I tried to lighten the blow for myself and say it was not that much work that needed to be done. The list kept compiling, soon I may yank my hair out in a frisson of stress. A glass of fine whiskey like the rich drink at leisure sounded good right about now.

"Top quality stuff ..." Maybelline speculatively said, as she wiped a finger down dusty window trim made from pine trees and stained with light stain to bring out the aesthetics. "Needs work, cleaning, painting, will take some time, Hank."

"Seen worse, May, I will take care of it and don't dwell. You do the cleaning, I'll do the repair, James will likely cry from lack of attention, we'll all grow from this experience." She looked at me like "yeah, yeah right, right... No ... I don't know" uncertainly.

"Nothing a little elbow grease can't fix, right?" Worst part was she had a mocking laugh that twisted my insides, I was trying here, I really was.

"Ah, shut it. You might as well play some music, change the records and dust the windows. I will grab a ladder and you can take care of the cobwebs. Spiders, yum … hope you're not afraid." I could see goosebumps, she chilled at the thought and revenge never tasted sweeter.

"I will not touch those cobwebs!" May bellowed adamantly again.

"Fine, fine, a man's gotta do all of the work or what?" I flicked her hair with a finger in a playful way.

"That is how it's supposed to be anyways, Hank, this house was your first choice." She knows how to grind my gears as well as read me, both go hand in hand at pissing me the hell off.

"Women are always bitching about equality, wanting to be treated the same as a man, then when the opportune moment arrives, you ditch out on the task. I could use a drink," I said, exhausted.

"That won't fix any of this." Straight to the point, dark and witty girl.

"Give me a break, will you, place needs more than elbow grease and more than we can afford to hire someone to do." I was making good money, that I was, but this took more than what I could possibly come up with on top of electric bills, water, house, the list goes on.

"I tried to tell you that,"–she did–"'the price was right' you said over and over again. There was a reason this place was affordable." Beat me down, beat me down she did.

"Go make some drinks, I will grab my tool belt."

"If you say so." Her lips soft against my rugged stubble-shadowed cheek, it was not five o'clock, but it sure as hell felt like it.

I struck a match off the dusty wood stove and smoked, smoked till my lungs burned, drank, drank till we cracked another bottle and I went to work. Maybelline played music, jazz, that beat, beat that made you want to dance right outta your seat. She sat and watched, I cleaned first, hammered down loose trim, ripped the carpet out before furniture was installed. Drove to town for paint and brushes, rollers, the whole nine yards.

19

Weeks and months were spent on the restoration of our home, a year came and went, James was three. The house was done, my handiwork, tools my dad let me borrow, and help from Damon on occasion got the job done. With Damon's help, we tackled the exterior, shingles, siding, and sealing off windows, painted too. Never do I want to paint anything again, May helped paint as much as she felt able too, another surprise came that limited her.

Maybeline was due for another kid, our second son was brought into this world two months after the house was completely restored, I named him Johnny after an old feller who used to teach me tricks with cards growing up, sharp chap as Johnny were to be one day when adolescence was in the rearview and he too was getting married and building a family of his own.

Damon and his wife came over and drank fine scotch, triple-distilled whiskey, rum, and vodka almost three to four nights of the week. We went out to the tavern in Carlton to be greeted as regulars by the old barkeep, he sent me a free drink or two at least each night. I was doing fine at work, still drank out back with the boys on break, sales were still hot and the money rolled in and went out in the mail for bills quicker than I could process.

The kids grew like weeds, James could talk some, but not much, Johnny just rolled around and beat his head against the crib if we were not keeping a close eye on him. I dealt with vomit more than a janitor at a bar, changed diapers, baby-powdered asses, potty-trained my eldest and told him how proud I was. My parents came over to visit and play with the kids on the weekend while I nursed a hangover with greasy food and television, and drank beer. I was getting older, not old, but older, more creases in my face, more age held behind my eyes, wiser.

20

My buddy Damon, well, at least he was ... See, when he was coming over for a while drinking, sometimes he would come without his wife, he would crash on my couch, drink my liquor, touch my record player, pat my kids on the head, help cook dinner, he was close, too close. What I later found out broke my heart in jagged bits and pieces and sent me down a road I would never return. It drove me insane, my hair luckily did not fall out, but my eyes were as cold and sharp as daggers, my personality was bitter, way too bitter for a father. I was cold, hard, shrewd, intelligible ... deadly.

Demons, mine did not chase me, I chased them with intention, piggy-backed all the way to hell and back nine times over. Hell on earth can make or break a man, I put up with more than I should've dealt with, more than most men would've. I was a fool in different ways, too kindhearted, forgiving, accepting. Damon, he, he never heard a word leave my mouth again. I hoped he rotted in the pits of hell where the beasts slaughtered victims and tossed the carcass of man and woman alike. The pits so sick a man, no, *an animal like him, belonged.*

I hoped he paid with more than just his pathetic excuse for a life. To turn the insides out of your best friend, I was his only friend, as far as I knew. We grew close as any would working together every week, drinking, smoking, and used to dabble in cocaine jointly at one time too. Tracks of jazz, blues, and, once in a great while, classical from Bach to

Beethoven, go to orchestras and witness symphonies. Playing pool, 9-ball was his favorite, that I remember. Now, his name, tarnished, a name I can't place a face to. I never truly knew him as well as I thought. Friends come and they go, sometimes stay, but mostly disappear.

Marriage is tough, rough, brutal in some cases, domestic abuse, you name it. I never beat my wife, touched my children, hurt them in the way I was hurt. Hurt, true hurt can be felt in your bones like arthritis, but it goes deeper than joints, the piece of you that beats as long as you are alive flares up in anguish. Abuse, your heart can be abused, taken advantage of, beaten, stomped on and run through the mud. My hurt goes deeper, my pain, my pain is unmistakable, it is visible in everything I do after what was done unto me.

When you make vows and are bound by marital contracts, paperwork that can cost hundreds, if not thousands, of dollars to file for a divorce. Leaving is a thought, a recommendation, I learn from my mistakes, this time not soon enough. The toxicity was viral, appeared in my movements, laugh, and fake crooked smile.

My wife was pregnant for the third time, to my joy, surprise, it was unexpected. Johnny hit his first birthday and James turned four a little while beforehand. Kids are angelic when they want to be, problems too, devious as any woman. One day when they realize all the hard work you put into raising them, to being the best that you can be for them, that is the payoff. If there were a payoff, it would be their realization of all your effort, and of seeing them grow to be adults. Having your own little family is the next best gratification to railing ecstasy with a room full of naked women.

May started to act distant, I was worried, not sure what the hell was going on, I was trying really hard to be myself, the same man she married, stressed as hell, but the same, you see. She was acting strange, peculiar, the vibes she sent were off, she drank through her third pregnancy and I could never figure out why. I tried to tell her to stop, once I diluted the tequila with water, Maybelline's new choice of drink. The doctor said drinking while pregnant was horrible for the child, now why would she do such a horrid thing. I asked many nights, once to her face, only to be smacked across the ear by a woman for nothing more than caring. She smacked me because she was mad at herself, May drank even more for disrespecting me when I was only trying to find a resolve.

Problems in a relationship can drive you nuts, mad, off the confounded walls. Sad to say, I started to lose it on more than one occasion. The kids never saw it, they were too young to see their daddy be big, bad, and fierce. May was smoking cigarettes back to back, really chain-smoking those suckers down like a drunkard at the bar who forgot ten seconds later he had already smoked one. As an avid book reader, I read about children, development, birth, pregnancies, I knew the harm that could cause the infant while in the womb, lack of oxygen and all from dragging cigarettes down to the filter. Disreputable actions not befitting a proper woman, mother, it made it hard to love her over those months, too hard at times.

Damon was acting differently himself, he had a devilish grin on his face at work throughout May's third pregnancy. He quit coming over and drinking with me, stopped talking to me as much when we were at work. I was clueless to what was going on, a damn fool. You think the best in people when you let them in your circle, I learn from my mistakes and I learned from this to be more cynical and skeptical.

Come to find out Walt, our third child, I raised him as that, even though he was not my kid. He was born and I did not even recognize him, he looked nothing like me. Maybelline and Walt shared features but me, no, not, nada—nothing.

Damon and Maybelline were getting close while I was passed out on more than one occasion in the master bedroom. I'd come home and Maybelline's hair would be in a tangled mess and I didn't know why, those days Damon, the son of a bitch, left the dealership early. Everything started to fall into place, the dominoes were knocked over and I was left to pick them up one at a time, a bullet to the head would have been the easy way out. My old man raised me to be better than that, stronger than that, we both may hit the liquor hard, but we are not cowards.

I was blind, deaf, dumb, tricked by my own wife, a whore, the love of my life committed adultery, rotten to the core. She stabbed me in the back 'til craters bled when she was the one who was supposed to be guarding it with her life, as I hers. With caution, I put her down with words like venom, salt on an open wound, dark as the devil's soul, hateful, hurtful, vile, I made sure she knew what she did, made sure she understood.

Walt, Damon wanted nothing to do with his child, nothing at all, like he was some abomination, when Damon himself was the abominable one. Despicable filth I would not even want to touch the bottom of my shoe. How could he do this to me, I asked, I asked and asked, no answer was given by anyone, I figured it out though. He was a salesman without a soul, like many before and many after. An older man too, apparently Maybeline was into that, I never asked.

Delilah was devastated by the news, I drove over one day and laid it out, a terrible thing for me to do, but I needed someone else to feel the pain I felt. She wept like a schoolgirl who found out her parents died while eating the peanut butter and jelly sandwich her mom prepared that morning before waking her up and giving her a kiss. Who was I to channel this, to cause her pain as Damon did to me, no Damon did to both of us, it was not me who caused this, it was the truth. The heart-shattering moment when you find out not only was your wife cheating on you, but pregnant with another man's kid and living under your roof you spent your hard-earned money on. When I lost Abe and Josiah all those years ago after our short friendship, when I lost my brother, I thought I knew pain, I knew agony, suffering, not until now. Mark my words, I said in years past that it could be worse, that nothing worse could be done unto me, I was wrong.

I should've knocked on wood, to be safe.

This became the start of true sorrow. I wish the alcohol would numb, I wish it would all go away, but it wouldn't. Most nights I was shaky, smoking a cigarette, my hair grew out, I combed it back with dirty fingers and long nails. I sat at the dining room table drinking from the bottle like a baby. I felt cold, detached, but my feelings for the most part were buried inside, deep down in the chasm where all my misery was held captive, a prisoner within.

21

Maybelline and I stayed together through thick and thin, the stunt she pulled was never gone, never forgotten, I quit making love to her from then on. We stayed together for the kids, I could've hung myself if I had the balls to try it again, but what life was that to live for my children who needed me more than ever. May was my dream girl, she was my first true love, the girl I lost my virginity to, the one I did everything with. We stared at the stars more nights than I could count on the hands and toes of five men and six women. Nights where we made love on the roof with the grit of shingles like sandpaper scathing, scraping at my back.

Evenings where we watched the sun go down over a glass of whiskey on the rocks, an occasional Manhattan, or her favorite, a mint julep. I knew more about that woman than her whole family combined, knew her inside and out, at least I thought, until she cheated on me with Damon. The man I did my first line of cocaine with, the man who got me a job, a good one too, the man who sold me my first car, repaired my house with me, and the man who fucked my wife.

Maybelline, oh Maybelline, why did you do it, why did you whore around with another married man, were your needs not met, the commitment not equal, what was it? I asked her night after night, drunk, belligerently drunk, my eyes red from exhausting all energy, red with hangover after hangover temporarily put to the side after I started drinking again. She would not say for the longest time, no matter how much I begged. I told myself a man doesn't beg, doesn't grovel, doesn't accept pity, so I stopped.

I pointed my handgun at my temple most nights, with one bullet in the chamber and a pound of pressure on a two-pound trigger, I couldn't do it. I danced with the devil and he taught me hideous things, showed me in my dreams, showed me waves of blood, ominous and foreboding. I was drinking too damn much, smoked two, maybe three, packs of cigarettes a day, my throat wore raw, stung when I swallowed. I brushed my teeth with vodka, drank absinthe for dinner to experiment with hallucinations unparalleled by that of any drug I had done to that date.

Yeah, she told me why, told me how come, why she did it, after weeks, months of more agony, raising a child that wasn't even mine. Taking care of Walt's rashes on his baby bun ass, wiped the shit from his leg, fed him with a bottle, told him I loved him every night. He filled the void along with my other two sons. The gap that was missing after Maybelline ripped out my heart. I would raise him as my own and no one, I mean no one, besides those who already knew, would know the dark secret.

"Hank …" voice soft, innocent, her voice used to be, anyways. Now, now it was like rusty steak knives shoved in my ears, harsh death impending.

"What the hell do you want, May." My voice, shaky, betrayed, sloshy gargled words from drinking all day and night for days, months, I don't even remember it was that bad. The place where I bought my alcohol, Naps, they really knew me by name, even offered me a punch card, by twenty, get the next free.

I was on my fourth free one.

"You wanted to know," she had little Walt cradled in her arms, "why … I … did … it."

She used to make my heart skip beats from happiness, excitement, passion. What it skipped from at the moment was hurt, my eyes felt like they were bleeding as I started to cry. "Spit it out, spit it out already, you vermin! You've been hiding it for too long, what the hell do you have to say?"

"Damon … he was nice …" her words felt like a dirty knife stuck under my ribs, "he was a smooth talker and handsome, I was drunk, drunk past the point of no return–not conscious of what I was doing." Her head was angled at the floor in despair, the kind you get from making the biggest mistake of your life. "When he touched me and took me to the couch. I don't know why I did it, why I continued to do it." Raven black hair soaking up tears as it tickled her button nose.

"Hank, I love you–" I thought she did, but love does not consist of spewing acid on your husband's heart, and pissing on his name.

"Shut it, shut your filthy goddamn whore mouth!" I snapped at her like a dog beaten and locked in a cage. "You do not know love, you thought you once did, might have. I thought I did too, but it was fake, all fake. You defiled me, ruined what we had, I don't know if we as a couple could ever be right again."

She started to sob like I did when my brother died, I locked myself in a closet jam-packed with clothes, mothballs, and dirty tennis shoes. In a way, I knew her regret, if not from a different spectrum, I was contrite for being born, my birthday was the day my brother died and my birthday was the reason he died. May, she was the reason our relationship might die. Kids complicate relationships, if it were not for the kids, I would have thrown her out the door, split if she did not leave, signed the papers and been done with her ass. Or, I'd have gone on a one-way ticket to hell or a high-speed chase in the coupe, the results all the same.

"I was so drunk, so out of my mind, infidelity, atrocious … I'm so sorry!" She cried, tears dripped from cheek, to chin, to Walt's blanket-wrapped body, snot bubbles protruded from her nostrils. Monsters can cry too. I do not know how I feel about one holding my child, any of my children. It is imperative for a child to grow up with both their parents still attached and secure, safe and sound, steady. A bumpy road for a youngster can cause developmental issues.

"Drunk! What kinda fucking excuse is that!" Mocking her, I said, "Drink a little much, fuck a close friend of your husband, not only husband, but our FAMILY." I used to desist from cursing at her, but that was prior to the harm she did. "How does that justify anything, or how is that an adequate excuse?" Choking on air, nerves were kicking my ass. I sat at the dining table in our house, crying, shaky as a leaf in the wind. "You disgust me, you really do. Never once did I think of doing something like that to you. You know Delilah, she used to look at me–"

"STOP!"

"Women, many women saw me, wanted me–"

"Hank, stop, just stop!"

"I never pursued, talked, flirted–for you."

"But I was drunk, Hank, drunk I tell you–listen, DRUNK!" The littler ones started to whine, James was in his room on his twin-sized bed. She brought this up herself, I had no hand in this matter, no matter the implications, excuses, any of it. I was a good man, a good husband, a good father.

"You don't listen, leave me alone."

"But..."

"Go sleep in James' room with the kids, I want you nowhere near me." Words brutal, pitch and tone intermittent with brain pickled by liquor.

"Hank..."

Some things you just can't undo.

"Go." I had nothing more to say.

May took Walt and Johnny, black makeup streaked her face like a Jackson Pollock. I stayed at the table for hours, drank through a bottle as the sun came up over the valley. Bright and obnoxious, the sun burned my retina as I stared into its core, looking for answers in all of the wrong places. Where was I to look? The bottom of the bottle held no answers, only a short respite from tragedy, but in my drunken stupor I fell into a manic depression. A state I do not recommend, a place I did not want to go.

Deciding the couch was where I would sleep, the empty bottle was smashed in anger against a pine tree out back, the birdhouse fell to the ground and shattered as did the bottle. Sick to my gut, I headed back inside to the living room and flicked on the TV for something to take my mind off my troubles as I fell asleep.

Nightmares were waiting, ready to play their games, games my mind was strong enough to endure. Then I learned bad dreams can be good, depending on perspective. Under the right circumstances, terrors in the night can become a blessing in disguise.

That was what had come: good fortune.

22

Snoring, asleep, sound asleep, lights from the television flickered like static on channel three, the channel that played the–

"*BREAKING NEWS*," what… the TV … it speaks to me? "*Local McMinnville resident stabbed multiple times,*" huh … only miles away … manslaughter, "*domestic case, wife used a serrated kitchen knife to murder her husband.*" My eyes were glued shut, eyelids extremely heavy, equating to a ton of bricks, but I listened. "*Throat was slit, twelve puncture wounds to the torso and both arms were lacerated to the bone. Wife committed suicide as the police arrived, a bullet from a .38 shot inside her mouth and exited the back of her head.*" A woman's voice described a fantasy, a dream, no … no this was real, I looked with blurry eyes, a headache that beat like a drumline drummer. The swine that at one point in time was my friend was murdered and poor, innocent Delilah blew her brains out.

News, fantastic, out of this world but yet in this world. Karma, it's real, it has to be. The snake got what he deserved: Damon was murdered by his wife in cold blood at his house. Delilah is dead, but she went out with style, if I could thank her for doing what I couldn't, I would. But she is gone now, the same as Damon. No longer do I have to bide my time at work with him there to stir up memories. No longer would I have to sulk and hide behind his grin, the whispers abundant around the office, people would only remember his death, a death he deserved.

Poetic justice was only in the movies and novels, now, now it is factual.

Hours past the blissful news:

"I saw breaking news on the television, news my wildest dreams could not have made a reality," I told her, my wife, not that the traitor's death would make her hands clean or mine less scarred.

"What, what are you talking about, Hank?" Drinking from the bottle, licking my lips as if sugar sweet as cherry pie was upon them. May had Walt and Johnny on her lap, James was going potty like a big boy, the way daddy instructed him.

"News, amazing news. You missed, too bad, soon enough you will read the headlines, you too will see." Her expression quizzical, lost in my riddle, the words were bitter, but filled with thrill.

"Hank ... I have not seen you this excited since–" Since she broke my heart, I knew what she was going to say to me, though I did not care to let her finish.

"Exhilarated, like the first time I snorted cocaine! So surreal, yet so real."

"You are mad, I tell you, you have been drinking too goddamn much!"

"Me? No, just enough to deal with what you did."

"Please, you are scaring me…" Walt had no clue what was going on, Johnny tensed at his mother's fright, but did not cry to my surprise.

"You will understand, go run and fetch the paper, don't touch my car. I will watch the boys, now go," her eyes questioned my sanity, "shoo, do as I said."

"Why so urgent?"

"I want you to see why I am content," drinking vodka like sparkling water, no bite, lips puckered, I continued, "relieved, soon you too will understand."

"Watch the kids, alright."

"Ma Ma," James said as he came out of the bathroom to where we were speaking in the dining room.

"Daddy's going to watch you, James, I will be back shortly." She knew, she had to, her face turned grave. May knew the only thing that could turn my somber expression bright and I had not indulged in cocaine yet since James was born.

"Come here, James, sit down, I will make us some eggs ."

"Okay." He crossed his little arms, fragile and pretty, eyebrows raised, he looked to where I stood cooking.

Maybelline ran out of the door, our driveway was an exercise in itself to walk, let alone run, she made haste and was back in ten minutes. I had just cooked eggs and toasted slices of buttermilk bread for myself and a bagel infested with raisins for James. Johnny was crawling around on the ground like a dog scratching its ass, and baby Walt was in a jumper I set up in the arch of the doorway between the utility room and the kitchen. He bounced and bounced, oblivious and happy, happy as I was. His real dad was dead now and I was glad that he would never have to meet him. A replacement father, no need for adoption papers, potentially one day the truth would come.

"What ... oh ... my ... heavens." Maybeline was shocked as she unrolled the newspaper. "No ... no ... it can't be." Baffled, where I was ecstatic.

"Yes, oh, yes it can, I feel sorry for Delilah," adding negativity in my voice as if I were a teacher who returned an essay with errors and passing along sardonic advice, "your friend, co-worker. But what you did is on your hands, she is free now, free from the horror." Delilah was truly a sweet girl, I felt awful for her, yet relieved because as I said "she is free now."

"Uh ... umm ..." Now May was reading the fine print, the juicy details, as I placed both elbows on the table, fingertips of both hands touching in a wave, back and forth, back and forth.

"Yes, yes ... mull it over." Eating my buttermilk toast after spreading butter, I enjoyed it. James was unaware what was going on, probably for the better.

"Be ... cause ... of ... me..."

"You selfish girl, you can't take all of the blame. It was because of both of you." I started to laugh hysterically. If I could pay for this kind of entertainment, I would be broke as a joke.

"He ... and ... she, dead?" May dropped to both knees, covered her face in her dirty hands and prayed to whomever would listen. Who? Forgive her for what she had done, she deserved this.

"No use, get off the ground, get yourself together, we have a family to raise." Dead serious tone persuaded her to rise. Bumfooted to the kitchen, reach for the top shelf, where a multitude of liquor was kept in a make-shift cabinet. Her choice of poison was tequila, she poured a glassful to start her day, much as I. Except I was celebrating, she was coping.

"They died, both of them. How could I do this, how…" She took my insults with a grain of salt, knowing they would come until I felt it was not worth my breath. May had nowhere to go, this was her home and she knew better after her stunt than to fight back with words after the harm she dealt.

"Damon, throat slit, ah, what a shame. Should have been more vio-lent, your friend from work, Delilah, his wife. She should have cut out his eyes and shoved them down his throat, or better yet. chopped off his pecker and fed it to the rats." Casually, I said the words as if they were no harsher than a thank you to a waiter at a restaurant. When you are a sweet guy, girls tend to take advantage of you. Girls can take your still beating heart from your chest, like it was a mirage until the hallucination dissipates and you are left heartless and alone.

"She, I just saw her yesterday, and he. Both dead." May was lost in space, out of her mind, much as I had been lately.

"Yes, you have said that before. They are both dead. Gone. Terminated–for good." I had a tray with tobacco on the table, papers to the side and a poker I used to pack.

"Hey, throw me those filters, May." She sat across from me at the din-ing table, James was sitting on the side next to me in his highchair.

"Here," May's lousy throw resulted with the filters landing on my unclean plate, "Hank, does this mean we, we can start over again?" Her eyes like washed-up bottled glass from the sea, hopeful as the first time I lost myself in them. I used to be able to stare for hours, lay on the bed and gaze. That was before things changed drastically.

Laboring on my cigarette with care, I sprinkled a proper amount on the paper. With six fingers, three at each end I began to condense the tobacco, rolling up and sliding it back down. I licked the glue two thirds of the way and set it down to look at May, as I grabbed the filters from my dining plate, flicking her scorn. She waited for a response, good, she could wait, I had waited for an answer for why she did what she did for far too long, only to get an inadequate story.

Pathetic.

Shoving a filter in one end, I licked and sealed, packed the tobacco with a poker from the opposite end, added more and twisted it to a point to finish it off. One hearty cigarette to enjoy. Lighting, I watched the paper burn smooth as it ignited the tip where I twirled it to a point like a unicorn's horn, seeing the rest burn slow, I feared that it was condensed far too much.

Placing my lips to filter, I took a drag, long and deep. The smoke came into me like a demon and came out raspy as I spoke, "You think this is your chance, leverage to right your wrongs?

"Why, so you can get drunk again and do it all over," adding for pleasure, "break me once more. Am I your toy to budge and break, lose and find again?"

"It's ... it's not like that, Hank!" She drank her tequila with haste. The newspaper was discarded in the trash along with other worthless garbage. For some reason, I wanted to remove the paper from the wastebasket, grab thumbtacks and tack it to the wall where she could see it every damn day, clear as day like the image that hides behind my eyes at the forefront of my mind; my wife in bed with another man.

"You want what you want because you are a fool too." The liquor was hitting me hard, sick from a hangover and on another bender, I felt between worlds.

"No, Hank, I love you!" Her eyes moved over to our son, what great examples are we, sitting at the table for all to see. "James, go to your room, please, your father and I are speaking like grownups, please, privacy."

"But mom. I want to stay here with you," his lovely voice could make angels cry. Johnny was roaming the living room on his own accord and Walt, Walt was bouncing like a pogo stick in the hands of a hyperactive kid.

"Just for a moment, son. Your mother and I have to speak and it is better now than later," speaking firm and unwavering. James got up after pinching my arm and giggling as he walked by to head to his bedroom.

Rolling another smoke before we got back to our discussion, I tossed it down the length of the table to May, I was still nice in some ways, not most, but some. She grabbed a matchbook and ripped one out to strike and set her cigarette aflame. May puffed to get the cherry going and exhaled with eyes leaking tears for me and not the smoke drifting up.

"What is it that you want from me? I am a good father, better than some and not more than most. I am honest, kind, at least I was. What more can I have to give you if what I already gave was not enough?"

"You gave me everything, I was the foolish one. I was not naive, Hank, I'm sorry for being a bitch and causing all the pain I did." Her lips pressed against glass for a gulp, smearing the remnants of red lipstick she had on the night before as she always does.

"Honest, your words are they true?" How could I ever trust her again, maybe learn to down the road, but that would take some time. To stay together for the kids would be worth the endeavor.

"Is it greedy of me to want to right my wrongs?" She sounded sincere, nevertheless cross-examination was never my strong suit. Knowing her for years and the deceit I had not detected was evidence enough.

"Yes. Yes, it is. To fix our family for our children, they must never know what happened. What you did, I do not want them to grow up knowing you were a whore." I made her cry–good. She had yet to pay back all of the misery she had caused.

"Quit, Hank, stop calling me that."

"Whore?"

"Stop, please," May's voice was a whisper as she implored.

"Why, that is what you have shown. To sleep with two married men, I didn't even know through your entire pregnancy. Walt is not my son by blood." The liquid in my veins, abrasive from vodka and anger, evidence present in the tone of my voice and the severity.

"I am a whore." Second-guessing herself, "I was. Does that make it better?" She tucked her hair behind her ears to deny the tears, a sponge, smashed her cigarette in a ruby red ashtray made from plastic composite.

More tears fell down her cheeks. I pitied her like a homeless man who pleaded for change–there was no love lost.

"That is a start, what if the roles were reversed here, May, what if I was the one fornicating. How might you feel? Would you feel jubilant as you looked at me, might you feel open-hearted?" My wife knew I had a point, that I was in earnest aroused by her displeasure at my words sniping at her.

"No, no I would not. I would hate you, hate your guts, despise you as a human being and my husband. You are the real salesman here, I cannot sell you myself better than a pitch you might create, I can try my best, though I am not sure if that is good enough." We sat and drank, I was sedate, drinking, taking my time without bother. She knew I was the alpha, you go against the head wolf, you will be lucky to walk away with your life. These were mere superficial bites.

"You better try now or live as a ghost," reminding her, " I will see you as that."

"I love you, Hank, even though you will not say it anymore, I love you. I love the way you look at me, the way you smile and laugh at me, the way your affection makes me feel alive. I love your love, it's like a drug.

"Our honeymoon was nothing but laughter. Non-stop drinking and celebration with walks on the beach with sand between our toes. The sunset was beautiful, best enjoyed while in your arms. I miss you holding me, loving me, caring for me–"

"I care for you, dammit!" I snapped, hand placed against eyelids as salty liquid crawled down eyelash to splash and splatter on the table's varnished top. "I did not stop caring for the woman I fell in love with. But you, now. I have no idea who you are, who you have become is not the girl I knew."

"Hank, I am still the same woman. Inside and out, I make mistakes, terrible mistakes. I have become the sniveling by-product of those mistakes. Look at me now," swollen eyes and a bleeding lip from biting hard, the way I used to bite it when we were making love, "I am a complete mess."

Caustically, I told her, "No, no, you are not a mess. You're fine, don't worry. You have nothing to worry about, put me through hell and relax."

"Look, alright, I swear I will make this up to you–"

"How!" I lashed back with my fists smacking the table, the little ones whined, they would not remember this moment, they were too young.

"Anything. Absolutely anything you want," she said solemnly, afraid to look at me now.

"Be who you used to be and expect nothing in return from me, do not be fake, be yourself again. Do not cheat on me ever again or I will cut your traitorous tongue from your mouth.

"Raise our children with me, be there. They need us both, do not ruin this."

"Yes! Yes, I can do that. I understand."

Maybelline dropped her head in crossed arms and cried for hours, I drank and rolled cigarettes, smoked and read poetry while she wept.

With faith in our family, I'd bet money we would get through this, not that I could ever love her again the same as before. My lips would never let the words "I love you" leave them for her again while she is alive. Mark my words. When you have children, you know just as I have found out, you go to great lengths to make sure they have a better life than you had. I want to give my children opportunities, I want them all to go to the college of their choice if they wish, to have cars and a welcoming home, a family, and a few close friends to boot.

I want them to have the life my brother never got to have.

23

With my spare time, I started to write a lot of poetry, some got published. I started to make a name for myself in the area and the paper. Working for the car lot still selling automobiles, knowledge and material was attained through my work, to enhance my writing. Sell what you believe and the great patrons will flood in to buy it, write what you believe and those patrons will read and comprehend, feeling your pain, love, happiness and tribulations.

Mom and Dad were still kicking strong, I took Damon's more prestigious place in the office and accrued twice the money I had when starting. Ten years of saving money and paying on the house until it was paid off, May put down her fair share as well and we lived in peace. I did not show affection the way I used to, we did not have sex and definitely did not make love. She would sneak a kiss on my cheek and sleep on the mattress with two feet in the middle of space. I was hurt and ten years did not fix that.

Investments in stock were paying off and I was comfortable, more than the chaps I ran into at the bars. I went out and drank by myself, once in a blue moon I would drink with Luis, who was now the police chief in Carlton, seeing how the last one had a heart attack screwing a hooker in his cruiser. Luis and I drank whiskey and played pool, chatted about sports we hardly watched and drank beer while staring at girls' asses. I was still hitched to Maybelline, but considering everything, I did not deny myself the pleasure of checking out women.

"You got smokes?" Luis looked at me through heavy eyes with bags beneath, I had talked him into grabbing drinks after he worked a double shift.

"Depends, what you got for me, Hank?"

"Quarter?"

"That'll do." He was a good guy, like me, better than most. Fair too, if I might add, we would pay for smokes and buy drinks for one another, it all equaled out and that was dandy.

"Look at the rack on her, pal." I angled a rough finger to the girl who passed us as we sat at the bar, I lit a cig and blew smoke into the aisle.

"Doubles, you know I like 'em that way."

"We both do."

"Hey, don't you have a wife?" He knew, but asked nonetheless.

"I do, don't you?"

"Yes."

"And?"

"I never told you this, but we are swingers."

Jaw-dropping, miraculously, my smoke still resting in the corner of my mouth, must've been saliva that glued it to my lip. "You mean you're allowed to have sex with other women and she, she sleeps with men," emphasizing the men part, like her taking more than one guy's dick was abnormal.

"Strange in this day and age, trust me, I know. My wife and I live a peculiar life, distant and close, depending on the time. Strange lovers, man, strange lovers."

"Luis, that'll seem strange any day and age, I am sorry."

"It's okay, Hank, we are just wired differently than others sexually."

"No kidding, I've heard of porn stars having husbands and vice versa."

"We don't film, if that's what you are asking."

"Hell, what do you take me for Luis, some kind of perv?"

"Bastard, I could ask you the same thing. Another drink, buddy?"

We had been sitting at the tavern in Carlton for twenty minutes, my coupe was parked out the front door and damn did she look as good as any woman that had walked through that threshold tonight. May was watching the kids while I had some of my own time, after over a decade of marriage, you need small intermittent breaks.

"We taking shots or your ass want cocktails?" I asked.

"On the rocks or...?"

"Take my spirits neat, partner, right off the shelf."

He nodded and got our barkeep's attention, since Luis issues the vast majority of tickets in town, our drinks came quick. "Here you are, Hank."

"You're real sweet, you know that."

"Keep it shut or I am going to detain you for public indecency."

"What the hell you mean, Luis, my pants are up and pecker stashed away."

"Not when I pants you for the lot of them to see in here how tiny that pecker is and whoop your ass with my baton."

"That some kind of homosexual joke, I'm straight. I know you swing–"

"Pushing my buttons now, Hank, you know I was only joking. I'm as straight as any."

"Yeah, okay. Damn, did you see that?"

"What?"

"That lady over there with the blonde hair and big eyelashes," I pointed to help my blind friend, "for being a cop, your eyes aren't very sharp."

"Hey, look, Hank, before you miss it," I turned the opposite direction, falling right into his trap.

"Ow, what the hell." Luis had his fist next to my face so when I turned, it got me right in the eye.

"I saw it with my own two eyes, Hank–you ran into my fist."

"I'd call for help, but the asshole on duty is sitting here drinking with me."

"Cleveland is down at the station taking calls, sure he would come watch you be clumsy and hit your face on my fist."

"I'm sure he would. See, Cleveland ain't worth a damn, so I would save myself the quarter for the call." Cleveland, the new deputy, trainee, whatever the toddler is, is not worth the sperm his father wasted on that dumb son of a bitch.

"Had to hire him, no one else wanted the job." Luis swirled his whiskey around to get a better whiff, then swished it in his mouth while he contemplated his disappointment for Carlton's police force, like many before. Shame, it really is.

"Do not blame them. Working under you would be the next best thing to blowing dick like the hooker you never arrest, because she cuts you in for a discount, being chief that is."

"If you did not run your mouth, I would think you might have died. What'll you do one of these days when someone pops you in the teeth for being such an ass, Hank?"

"Probably call your ass like most these pansies who can't back up what they say."

"I like that, my job would be so much easier if guys had balls. Whatever is down there is far short of necessary."

"You said it, cheers." We smacked glasses like they weren't delicate.

Stayed around the bar for a few hours, drinking and talking. My face got warm and tingly, the kids were running around the house making a ruckus, I knew. Taking a break was nice, let me compartmentalize my thoughts about my poetry, add more material for me to discuss at a later date. Eventually, Luis and I smacked each other in the balls and went our separate ways, he took off in his cruiser, swerving like any other drunk. They don't pull you over in Carlton for that, speeding is one thing, swerving is an expression. I took off the opposite way and headed back to the kids and wife, three boys are a lot of work. My parents had two, I see why they started spanking our behinds first and asking questions second.

24

"You have fun with Luis?" She asked, sitting on the couch in a robe, the kids had gone to bed a few hours ago, apparently.

"As always, I had a damn good time."

"That's good, you want me to make you something to drink?" Lacking any lingerie beneath, I knew what May was up to. She was trying to seduce me. We did not argue about spilt milk, however I abstained from sex to that day and saying I love you was not part of my vocabulary. I wonder who it was harder on, her or me.

"What time is it?" As if it mattered, it was the weekend and I had no clock that dictated what I wanted to do.

"9:30, you want to do something?" she said it sexually, I felt differently.

"The night's still young, let's go to Portland." I was ready to party and have a good time.

"You want to go to that bar down Hawthorne where they make spicy Bloody Mary's?" Maybelline was intoxicated herself already, more so than I. If she was trying to seduce me that meant she was watching those romance shows on TV, dreaming about me taking her again. Who knows, after a decade, it might be time. For one thing, I knew that desisting from any sexual intercourse was worse for me than cigarettes.

"Yeah, sure. What's that called, 'Mexico City'?"

"Right, that's it. It has been a while, Hank." She was referring to me taking her out, it had been. For fun I left her at home, she could go shopping if she liked, we bought a baby blue pickup she was fond of. After Delilah died, May kept herself from making any friends, she worked and focused on the kids.

"Go freshen up, I will tell James he is in charge until we get back."

James willingly took charge with glee. I headed to the bedroom after walking through the bathroom where Maybelline was changing, naked and ravishing as the first time I saw her sparkle. Releasing the main drain with relief while she touched up her makeup, she only shook her head.

Behind my desk, I had placed under a window in the bedroom where the old oak scratches at the glass, I grabbed my revolver to place it in a holster under my leather jacket. I had sold my Beretta years back to a pawnshop and upgraded to a 45. Sliding paper from a pack on the desk's side, I inserted it in my typewriter to write a poem before we left. Poetry exudes when you are as drunk as I.

"You ready?" Placing pearls over her earlobes and clipping them in the back, she asked me at my desk.

"Yeah, yeah, I am. Let's go."

Drinking on the way, I had a fair amount straight from the bottle. We listened to jazz, as I always do. It was 11:00 p.m. by the time we made it to Hawthorne, groupies huddled in front of Mexico City. I grabbed a cigarette from a pack in Maybelline's purse and lit it with a deft movement of lighter and hand. The front door had a bodyguard checking ID's, big Mexican with a gut on him like a pig.

"Cabrone, ID," he said.

"Can you not tell I am older than you?"

"Puta, you too," the guy was not budging and whatever he was calling us was not English. I spoke Spanish when it required me to order a beer, that was it. Cerveza is my word and I use it frequently.

"Fine. Here." We showed ID and got the hell in there before I decked him in his throat for being such a bastard.

The music was wild, not jazz and not American. Our barkeep was a short Hispanic lady with black hair like charcoal, she came up and was polite enough to speak English. "What will you have, ma'am? Gent?"

"Two Bloody Marys and double shots of tequila," May ordered, there she went, going for the tequila. I seldom comprehend or remember well after drinking that crap. What the hell, tonight's a night to drink.

Dancing was a hobby we both did collectively back before May cheated on me, I did not touch her. We were only friends really, I loved her and desired to have her in sensual ways, but I had restrictions. Alcohol was a bad influence when it came to sexual urges, I could control myself, but tonight we might rekindle that fire.

Just maybe.

"You want to dance?" She asked with bashful eyes and a shot of tequila sterilizing her mouth.

"To this shit?" As if it were an insult. There were maracas banging away, I like jazz and some classical, this was trash in my opinion. "Opinionated prick" is what I get called at work, don't like it–tough.

"Well, if you don't want to, that is all you have to say." Maybelline was getting moody, she ordered more shots and a second bloody Mary, my insides felt like a nuclear war went off.

"I don't want to."

Recklessly, I drank down four shots of tequila and did not know what the hell was going on. It was 1:30 a.m. and the bar was packed, I threw another cigarette in my mouth and started to smoke. May copied and lit her smoke off the candle on the table. The noise was getting to me, that and the tequila and all the alcohol I had consumed.

Drunk and out of my mind, I got up with a lame right leg, buckling from lack of proper balance. Holding onto the back of the chair I had been sitting in, I looked at May, "I am going to the bathroom, stay here." She nodded and sipped her tequila down. For years, she had been putting down a quart a day, starting early in the morning. At this point she was a professional.

Cruddy bars and sketchy people, they made one hell of a drink here though, I'd give them that. Approaching the bathroom, there was a Mexican man, about the same skin tone as my pal Luis, "Aye paisano. ¿Tu quieres cocaína?"

I kept walking, not knowing what the hell he was talking about.

When I started to push the door into the bathroom, he said again to me, but in English, "Aye, ese you want some cocaine?"

I looked back at him, now he had my attention. Bad habits always come back, I was three sheets to the wind. Coke might help bring me out of my stupor, "Sure, yeah sure, how much?" He walked up to me, black cowboy hat on with long black hair down to his shoulders and a mustache twisted to a point on each end, he was five-three, if that.

"Twenty, jefe." The mystery man of the night, my dealer pulled out a small clear plastic bag with enough for a party in it.

"Is the quality good, not cut with shit?"

"Clear ese, not mixed with nothing. Pure."

Grabbing a twenty, he saw my revolver and decided stiffing me and taking my money with a knife held at my throat was not the best choice. Smart boy. I had practiced almost everyday with Billy for the last ten years with my aim, I could draw faster than he could pull that crooked shiv of his out to play.

"Thanks, now piss off," I told him. Walking into the bathroom, I snorted a fraction of it while smoking another cigarette I pulled from behind my ear. Nobody came into the bathroom, my nose bled a minute amount, oh, well. I took a leak for what must have been five whole minutes, proceeded to wash my hands and exit back out to my wife.

When I got there, she had some darker male speaking to her, I was pissed already. He walked away when he saw my eyes bore down to his soul and threatened to strip it from him like gum off a sidewalk. A woman at a bar by herself was an easy target, the fact she did not shoo him away had me unnerved. The cocaine was doing me right, out of my mind, but awake.

"Here, another one, Hank." With a double of tequila in front of me, I bit a lime and licked salt, threw it down the hatch and bit more lime and licked salt. I did it twice, I hated tequila.

"Your nose, it's bleeding, here let me wipe–"

"No, it's fine, I got it." Taking a handkerchief, I dabbed at the blood, staining the white material red in two places.

Drinking more, May and I were having fun, relaxing a bit. Maybelline kept eyeing me down, I would too if I were her.

Later the guy who sold me cocaine came over to my surprise, I thought of kicking at him so he would walk away, but decided not to.

"Aye, show us a trick, jefe." I looked at him incredulously, was this some sort of carny lingo I did not pick up?

"What do you mean, squirt?" Whether he was insulted or not. I was unsure, afraid of getting stabbed, I kept a close eye. Mexico City was one of the most popular clubs/bars of its time down Hawthorne.

"With the pistol, you can shoot, right?" Drunk as hell, I was not in the right mind to discuss my prowess, but I did anyway.

"Bet your ass, Cabrone." I had no idea what that word meant in Spanish at the time, the guy at the door said it to me. My new little friend glared at me, not a big deal, he could be pissed all he desired for all I cared.

"Cocaína, bet you what I have left against what you have for a trick." His tongue was slick, persuasive. I could win, money, drugs, yeah. Maybelline was busy looking at his hand when the guy showed a wad of cocaine.

"Hank, are you …"

"What?"

"Without me again. Give me some." I handed her the cocaine, she inhaled it right out of the bag.

"What sort of trick are you wanting to see for that?" I pointed at his abundance in cocaine.

"Shoot your shot glass off of señoritas head." May was high and looking at me with excitement.

"Let's do it, Hank, look at that, you see how much he is willing to lose." As if she knew already I was going to win. I was a good shot.

"I don't know, May, seems awfully risky." The little Mexican dealer looked at me, waiting, he had two friends with him at his hip like dogs.

"Hank, we should, you can do it."

"I, I just don't know."

"Hank," she stood up, had the double shot balance on her head, "do it, do it, do it," chanting me on as if we were at a frat party instead of this ghetto bar.

Looking from her over to the drug dealer, I asked, "From how far away?"

"From one end of the bar to the other." He grinned, thinking he would win, I would show him.

"Come on, Hank, let's do it. You can do that." May's reassurance did motivate me to win the cocaine. "Hank! Hank! Hank!" She was rowdy when on cocaine, really, really rowdy.

"Alright, alright, fine." The dealer moved people out of the way, everyone was watching now, with music blasting in the background and florescent lights flashing.

Maybelline walked down to the other end of the bar, I pulled out my revolver and engaged the hammer, without thinking, drunk off tequila, high for the first time in many years, out of my mind, I pulled the gun up and it was like slow motion.

"*BANG*" The bullet rocketed through the air.

Cocaine from both parties was on the seat I had been sitting on, the little man grabbed both bags and ran out the door. People swarmed and flooded to escape, I did not bother to run. The barkeep was calling an ambulance in broken English. It was futile, it all was. My mind was racing, what had happened, what the fuck did I do?

"May! MAYBELLINE!" I screamed, running down to her, it all happened so fast. Blood was leaking out in a steady flow from right below the hairline, I plugged it with a finger as if that would work. Pressing my lips against hers, they were already cold and lifeless, I tried to force air in her lungs to no avail. Maybelline was dead. My wife, the mother to my children, the lady whom I hated for the last ten years, but beared with for the sake of our spawn.

"I love you," the words drained out of me languid and slow. I buried my head in her breasts and cried. Maybelline had no idea what hit her, dead the instant the slug sunk into her brain and sprayed matter across the room. A pool of blood started to form around her black as night hair, the warmth zipping away from soft skin.

Sorrow leaves you weak and hollow.

It had taken ten years for me to forgive her for cheating on me, screwing my best friend. I guess I was right, saying I would not tell her I loved her as long as she lived.

That was what it took, death.

25

Laying on the floor with Maybelline, knowing I would be taken away and this, this was our last time together on this side, for soon she would be buried. The barkeep was only doing her job calling in the incident. I wasn't mad at her, she saw what happened and knew that it was just a bad situation all the way around. I tossed her a hundred and fifty dollars I had left in my pocket, she gave me a bottle of whiskey and one of tequila and took the rest for tip. I sat and drank, drank tequila for May because it had been her favorite for some time, and I drowned myself in top-shelf whiskey. Telling her stories and what I liked most about her, I had been hard on her since she broke my heart and now I felt grief like I can't explain.

I lost the girl of my dreams, one way or another.

Maybelline left a hole in my heart when she committed adultery, I thought that was the worst it could be, no, no this was far worse. She died and took half—we shared everything equally—left me with enough to survive, but she took the bliss. The perspective I have, the screwed perspective I assure no one desires to have—killing your wife, killing a man, your brother died on your birthday, two friends dead at your side— it comes with a price, the memory alone encumbers you, hops on your mind like a saddle and yanks on the reins, makes you fight to live. Life is always a testament of will; having the volition to make it to the pot to piss in, in the morning, go to work, feed your family, sustain your home and the land around it.

We are invariably fighting, sometimes we just don't know.

Arrested and handcuffed within an hour, the cops came in and looked at my pupils, if I did not die from alcohol poisoning, the cell they would put me in would kill me. Police bombarded my last drink with my wife, snared me like a rabbit and dragged me out the door, loaded me up in the back of a cop car, hands cuffed and hooked around my ankle. The fat one took my revolver and I knew I would never see it again. I was taken to the precinct and told them an account of what happened.

I made a call. My only friend Luis flicked his sirens on and ran lights to get to my side as fast as possible. Him being a small town cop, he had no weight to throw around, they only laughed at Luis.

Vomit sprayed the table and onto the floor, got on my chin and into the sheriff's sandy bowl-cut hair. Towels of white made of cotton were brought to clean the scene in our small 10 by 8 room. Yet again I gave an account of a horrible crime, this time, however, I was not allowed to walk away for murder in the first degree. After my trial they sent me to Salem, an hour away from my house. There I would serve my sentence at Four Way correctional facility off to correct my wrongs and make myself a better man.

Luis fought and fought for me to be acquitted, "I deserved this" I said, "just let me be."

26

A week later, I was able to get my hands on a newspaper, which was offered on account of the incident. I was in my cell, a cell lacking amenities and stained with mold on old mortar cracked by age and vibration from all the bellowing at night. "I didn't do this," they would say, and I'd tell them "Quiet, goddammit, quiet I am trying to sleep, if you did not do what they say you did, you will be out sooner than me, let the longtimer's catnap, you inconsiderate bastards," the begging would continue regardless, so I kept quiet most nights and hummed to the sound of jazz that never bailed out on my subconscious.

Inmates shared one copy of the newspaper. To my dismay, there were hundreds of inmates. By the time it got to me, the paper was folded a dozen times over and torn at a corner. In bold black ink the headline read "*William Tell Act, Mexico City*" My name had been listed below a picture of the scene at Mexico City bar. I was labeled as a crackpot, alcoholic, and cocaine cowboy carrying a .45 who thought he knew how to shoot.

The guy I shared my cell with interrupted my reading with his ill-waited impatience, "Hey, pass it over here."

"I made the front page, give me a moment, Marique." That was his name, strange, he said he was a part of a tribe from Africa. Marique's skin was black as the pieces we used for chess, the pieces he hand-carved in his spare time. With one arm, he was more vulnerable than I at first thought, but no one bothered him because he did the books for gambling. I said to him if he needed someone to have his back, I would. A friend, that is what I needed here.

The newspaper did one of two things, it let everyone in here know why I had been locked away if they were smart enough to put two and two together. And two, it stirred up the memories I was likely never to forget.

27

Where Maybelline went, I do not know, the life after this still eludes me. Her final resting place was at the old cemetery outside of Yamhill. I knew the grave well, even though I was not allowed to attend, mine was right next to hers, we invested in those years prior. Not knowing we were going to use them so soon, well, she. I felt as if I had abandoned her, left her for an unforeseeable future beyond this realm and into the next.

She died with many years left to live, died at a young age before wrinkles could become an issue, before her veins thick and clogged with tar from cigarette smoke and brain-riddled with holes from alcohol, before she had to acquire help getting out of bed or driving to the market, before she was able to see her children have their first date or graduate.

May died without me, you think or hope you die at the same time, die together and face what's next as a unit. No, it does not happen that way, one dies first and you are left to mourn, stuck with grief "I should have done this and I should have done that."

Wherever Maybelline had gone, she went without me.

We used to watch the sunsets when our fire was lit, before the tragedy, before the deceit. I'd like to think she ran off into the nearly perfect sphere of hot plasma; the star that brightens this planet. Not waiting for me one day to follow, to have her move on as I know I should to survive in this world. The stars at night long ago were a sight we shared, along with alcohol and packs of smokes. Now we share a last name in time to be on both of our tombstones, we share kids and memories that die with age. And I, I look at prison bars and see her walking by, taunting me, tantalizing, and I don't know why.

Sentenced to twenty-five years, my penance. Good behavior was not on the table, if I wanted to get out early, I had to die. To protect myself, I kicked a lot of asses, took shivs from fellow prisoners and stabbed them first, I was quick and could fight for an older man. It has been fifteen years since steel bars became my TV and a bunk bed with a paper thin mattress and featherless pillow became my sleeping quarters.

My children do not answer my letters, they were all sent to live with my parents when May died. Mom and Dad both passed away within a few years of me inadvertently killing my wife, the kids were sent to foster homes and all three graduated high school. Maybelline's parents were too decrepit to raise kids, they outlived my mom and dad, but shortly thereafter, died. Luis comes by once a week to visit and tell me what I've missed, he works hard and takes care of his family. When he gets a chance, he snaps a few photos for me from outside.

James and Johnny, Walt too, I have sent them a letter a week since I have been locked up. No replies, I do not blame them, for I caused their devastation by shooting their mother at a crappy bar. I left them to fend for themselves at a young age, and without a father to guide them through tragedy and its byword, life. They are doing good, Luis keeps tabs and takes pictures for me to see, my own secret agent for free. Walt works at a gas station in Carlton next to the bar I drank at for many years, James writes for the Yamhill County paper to my delight, Johnny took after his old man and has a job in sales at a Japanese car lot across from the steel mill in McMinnville.

I think often of life and how it has changed, how being trapped in here has driven me mad. They do not give me any medication that helps. Potato shine puts me to sleep at night, I help Marique out with our business inside the walls, the business we started eight years ago. Dealing cigarettes, alcohol, and drugs. Since I had experience in sales, he said I would be a good con man, we had a fixed price down the middle and anything off the top I could keep. I'd drink a third of a bottle before sale, take five cigarettes for every pack, and drugs I did not tamper with at first. That was until we started getting opium, I smoked it from a tobacco pipe I traded half a block of cheese for. It hides inside the support of my cot, a metal pole with a rubber garment I take off every night. Marique said opium would help, with the nightmares, it would help take away my pain. If only for the night. He was right, alcohol tastes good, but forgetting everything for the night takes precedence.

"You're getting old, Hank," said Marique.

"You are not that young yourself, one day you will be as old as me." I am fifty-three years old and counting.

"Ah, by then my balls will be stepped on and all the pretty young girls will think I am rich." He knew I had money, my parents inheritance, their place and the severance I got from Ford along with my stock had me sitting pretty at this point. All three of my kids did not accept any money I offered in the letters if they would just reply.

"You get out of here alive and I'll buy you a car to take those pretty young girls around in, Marique," I jested.

"You're full of shit. Hank, you stingy codger."

"I'm serious this time."

"You said that last time we had absinthe and drank it all to yourself, what was that you said—"

"I didn't want to waste a drop."

"That really hurts," Marique said with sarcasm.

"Next time I'll share."

He bobbed his head, "See that you do, would you like to play a game of chess?"

"Do I have to use one arm?" I flicked him crap, we did that. Spending 365 days a year with someone can make you close.

"Bite me, you want to be white or black?"

"Is that some sort of test to see if I am a racist?" I asked, pretending astonishment, we were sitting out in the yard on a stone bench that overlooked the convicts and guards up above in their watchtowers.

"Depends on which you chose." He handed me the white pieces before I could answer.

"I wanted to be black."

"No, no you don't. Not in this day and age." He looked at me with the most sincere eyes that would make a woman cry. Some southerners had taken his arm for being black and he almost died, after beating them to death with his severed arm like a bat. That was part of the story around the yard anyhow.

"Fair enough." We started to set our pieces up.

"Just because Martin Luther King gave his speech does not mean the war is over, it does not mean that we are as free as white men and women. We will always be hated by someone for our skin, for being different. The way of life can be remorseless," Marique was missing a tooth on the bottom and had three silver caps on the top and one to the bottom in the front that shined with spirit as the sun beamed overhead.

"The way of life can kiss my ass, your move."

"Your wife, does she still haunt you in your dreams?" He moved his knight out from behind his wall of pawns.

"Every night, even with the opium. She asks me how I do, how are the kids as if I can see them every day. She asks me to forgive her for what she had done, the infidelity. Then her teeth extend out like a switchblade and she chases me, running through our house on Old Mac Hwy." He nodded and I made my move to open up my queen so I could cut through his rook in two moves.

"Does she still beat at the bars of our cell?" In prison we see our demons, they haunt us every night. Marique had a sentence of thirty-five years, by the time he made it out of here, I would long be dead.

"When I start to nod off, her face is always pale and blood leaks from the bullet wound on her forehead. She just stands there and watches. Enough questions for me, how about your son, Jamal, does he appear in your dreams?" Jamal was killed the day Marique had been stripped of his arm, the southerners hung his child before him. He was not fast enough to save his son, I felt bad for him, I really did.

"My sweet boy," he moved a pawn forward two spaces, "he does visit and calls me papa still. The dreams are vivid, opium is a blessing." We had enough opium to smoke every night, slowly the trade in here grew. The guards were in on it too, I would give them better prices than the inmates as a favor. At times Marique would roll them joints and send the joints in a white envelope out with the books when the cart came by our cell. Once a week, our deals would be delivered by Kowski the librarian, an old German with a scarred face and nappy hair no matter whether you caught him awake or sleeping; he had a small Indian cigarette held with his scruffy, chipping lips.

"Yes it is, thank you for all that you have done for me, my friend," I said as I took his rook before his negligent eyes.

He nodded a humble, vindictive nod. "Quick like a tiger, you took my rook. Hand me a smoke, Hank, please." I grabbed one for myself too, we did not have the luxury of filters on every occasion so these were harsh, potent with flavor as well. I tossed him a cig, grabbed my lighter from the striped black and white pants I was required to wear,

"Thank you, Hank, you are a good man." His silver-capped teeth bit down as I lit the tobacco.

"You mind if I ask you a personal question, Marique?" I bit down on a cigarette and used the light I was allowed to bring in, my lighter from the days at the track so long ago where I met Abe and his brother Josiah.

"Feel free, you do when the lights are out." In our cell we drank and smoked in the dark while we spoke late into the night. Some evenings we would speak of women with beautiful legs and tight skirts that accentuated their apple-bottom butts, or the short stories I wrote in my free time along with poetry. Sharpening my skills to this day, perhaps there would be a job for me yet, selling poetry and stories around the globe for all to relish.

"Do you miss it?" I pointed at his knotted sleeve where his arm would've been.

"Of course, I miss it, almost as much as being between a woman's legs." His lascivious grin made me chuckle.

"Well, I mean, does your mind still trick you to think that it is there, even though it ain't?"

SETH ALLEN MATHEWS

"More than you would think, when I first lost it and was in ICU, my arm itched. Peculiar indeed, feeling an itch where there is no arm. My brain re-calibrated soon enough, though I do get jealous."

"About?"

"Only one hand to jackoff with."

"That's not so bad."

"It is when your arm gets tired and you cannot alternate." I busted up laughing, Marique was serious, and not, at the same time. He pushed back cheetah-print, framed bifocals with a finger and eyed me like a hawk about to swoop in on injured prey.

"Damn, here I was being serious and you, you make a joke out of it," eyes watered as I spoke, Marique started to laugh now too, breaking from his act.

"Lightening the mood has been my specialty, you know."

"Oh trust me, I know, after fifteen years–I know."

He looked at me concerned and said with shock, "How can it be, again. No. Every time, you could not go easy on me just this once."

"Checkmate," I licked my lips and blew smoke over my slumped shoulder into the wind's current.

"Just once it would not hurt to let your friend win." He shook his head as I shrugged.

"That is life, life is not easy, not even this once. I will keep you sharp as a scalpel if you learn from my wisdom."

"Philosophical bastard."

Time out in the yard was up for the day, we went in to taste mediocre dinner in the mess hall where they played Johnny Cash, *Folsom Prison Blues,* for all to hear. I smacked my leg and stomped my foot, all sang along. Food was served: mash potatoes with thick jelly-like gravy, stale jello, sweet corn, a slice of rye with expired butter, and a serving of ham with more fat on it than my entire body.

It was 9:00 p.m. and the lights were out, I slept on the bottom mattress. Marique was tired of me hopping off the top four or five times a night to urinate (he had gotten used to my quirks and mannerisms over a decade, and I his). I had a bad bladder if that were a thing, education in

123

the field of anatomy has never been an interest, something about blood and the human body makes me ill.

Drinking "Pinot Nero" wine, looking at the bottle, I could see it had a pale translucent color, it tasted worse than it smelled, and it flared up sinuses like raunchy sour milk. That's it, wine was like drinking sour milk, gross. Evidently that is how it should be, as Marique informed me, it felt like gut-rot impending as it worked its way down, down, down.

"Out of all the drinks we scored these last few years, this is what we are stuck with tonight. Kowski could not have brought something less repugnant?" I asked my cellmate.

"For your information, the grapes that undergo the process of transmuting into Pino Nero are fragile and deal with numerous diseases to gain its exquisite flavor. Another reason we do not come across it very often, it is more expensive," Marique was defending a bottle of medium-priced wine I had no idea existed until earlier today. In years past, I drank port with May on occasion, she acquired a taste after the red wine we had on our honeymoon.

"Delicate, huh, sure, my balls are delicate, but that does not mean the ladies like the flavor, I do not see the difference here," I said, baffled.

His fingers were massaging his creased forehead, "When do you ever? You're a brilliant man, Hank, but as far as taste goes, you're rather old-fashioned."

"Okay, grape aficionado. Listen, I know this stuff is bang-up in your opinion, but mine, in mine it tastes like the bottom of a hog's trough when the sun has been cooking it all day."

Flummoxed, he looked at me, "Have you eaten from the bottom of a hog's trough?"

"Dammit, no–figure of speech. But, I can imagine it would taste like this," I said with disgust as if it were a euphemism, "fermented fruit."

Marique brushed back his hair with long yellow nails due for a clipping, "You feel it yet?"

"What, the sickness from this Pino?"

"No, the buzz?"

"No, not really."

"How much 'ave you drank, Hank?"

"A third." And I was struggling with that.

"Once you get to the halfway mark, you'll see." We each had a bottle of our own and two more at our feet, Marique was sitting on the floor with his legs crossed and propped against the brick wall.

"Wow, you know, I feel pretty good," I smiled drunk, had made it to the middle of the bottle and felt the after effects.

"Not bad now, eh?"

"No, Marique, you were right. Tastes better after you are intoxicated, hey, you want a cigarette?"

"Sure, could you light it for me?" he raised his arm and looked at it disappointed, "one hand an' all is sort of a bitch."

"Yeah, yeah, sure." I reached under my pillow, grabbed lighter and cigarettes, handed Marique a smoke, set the tip aflame, he exhaled and coughed like cancer was in season.

"Hit you right, didn't it?"

"What the hell you put in this one?"

"Reefer and tobacco: a spliff, partner."

"You're kidding, right?"

"Of course, hey, you know what I was thinking about?"

"What, women?" Marique said sardonically.

"Besides that." I rolled my eyes.

"Burgers?"

Rolling my eyes some more, "No, but now I am. I was thinking about that time you were drinking a highball and I smacked the bottom of your glass, you remember?"

"How would I not, it cleaned out my sinuses and had me wishing my other arm was lying around so I could beat you with it." He set his cig on the top of a cork stopper to keep it clean, balancing it so he could pick up his bottle and take a slug.

"Auld lang syne."

"Reminiscing again, are yuh?"

"Always and forever."

As we drank all of our wine, we ate jerky stashed from under my cushion and slices of pepper jack cheese that melted in my mouth, candy from Mexico with spices that made my nose water and my gut churn. Damn good times indeed, I dropped my opium pipe out of its hidey-hole and inhaled a hit or two, perhaps three. Marique snatched my pipe and attempted to do it himself, failing and dropping the cherry on his leg. I took it from him, loaded it and accommodated my friend.

We both smacked our heads hard, the lights went out and the dreams were unforgettable. May and my children were there with me at the Salem Carnival, we rode the rides, ran through the spook houses with carts you could sit on and push; won prizes at darts and balloons, the rings that never stick on empty soda bottles, and a BB gun game where I hit every target dead on. May stood up and begged me to shoot a glass off her head, I tried and she was hit right in the same spot, I snapped out of my dream as the guard rapped on my cell's bars with a wooden nightstick.

28

Gasping, I choked on stagnant air, there wasn't any damn circulation in this joint. Rolling to my side, I told the guard, "Kurwack, you nut, it's 8:00 a.m., lighten up, I was trying to sleep, dream of your wife bent over, you know, the usual."

Kurwack came back to my cage and beckoned, "Hank, you dirty old perv, the last action you got was when the Titanic sank." This guy and I would banter, nice fellow.

"Kurwack, if your eyes were straight and not as crossed as my fingers when I'm hoping Dilmer stabs your ass, you would know your wife is a hag," I added, "and no use to defend." Dilmer was as weird as they get, he perceived guards to be his victims from back in his serial killing days. He runs at them with a fork, fogged glasses as thick as two fifty-cent pieces and a stiffy. That was his prerogative, Dilmer knew better than to chase me down or I'd pummel his ass.

"Wipe your ass next time you start to talk, shit's covering everything you exhale. Your ass is talking 'cause your mouth knows better."

"That was clever, you ever see a one-arm guy break a nose?" Marique, awake and chiming in with pleasantries.

"No, Marique. Have Hank be the demonstration dummy."

"Kurwack, you sack of shit, how about I test it on you, snide son of a gun," I retorted.

"Let's take one of your arms, left or right?"

"How about you let me out of here."

"Can't do that, Hank, afraid an old codger and a one-armed man will show me their pugnacious tendencies."

Marique added, "We would too."

"Ha, ha. Seriously, let me out of here."

Kurwack opened the door and freed me, I slapped him on the back, thanked him for the laugh and humorous start to my morning. Marique came up beside me, we were on the second floor and showers were on the first before the mess hall. We went to take showers in prison as a pair, he did not wash my back or nothing, we are not fags. Some demented individuals tend to try and assert their dominance via you "dropping the soap," I avoid uncomfortable situations such as that, like my life depends on it. There are dullards you run into here that have a problem with black people, most of them know not to bother Marique or I, but not all.

An L-shaped wall had shower heads lining it every three and a half feet or every four squares of tile horizontally, for those that do not know prison measurements. Marique and I were both on constant lookout to make certain we weren't going to die a pitiful death in the showers. This day, in particular, was one of those days. Fresh meat, "greenies" as we call them, the ones that do not know how to respect one another, primarily skinheads, a band of three entered the showers, one had a swastika tattooed in blurry ink on his throat, the other had one over each eyelid, and the third had a swastika on his bare chest. All three approached naked, Marique looked at me concerned.

"I only have one arm, you know how predictable that is, they can see which fist I am going to sock them with from a mile away."

"You have two legs, don't forget. And stay back, throw the soap at one, if anything—just stay back. I told you, I have your back." New guys never get the memo until it is too late, I am one old man you do not want to fuck with when it comes to hand-to-hand combat. I've received my fair share of scars behind bars, some mental and some physical. You learn from cuts, broken bones, contusions, it builds character.

"You better leave, old man, that coon is on his last limb," said the one with a throat tattoo of a swastika.

I glared, I was pissed. You do not go around flinging racist remarks near me, period. Subsequent to Abe and Josiah's death, I vowed that I would not let another friend die as long as I lived, I planned on keeping that. "Peckerwood, step back out of here, take your inbred buddies along with you. I know you are new around here, the three of you, if you want to survive, it's best you walk away. Put some clothes on too, for Christ sake, or better yet," I looked over at Marique, "go play whack-a-mole with your hard-ons."

"Hank, you just don't know when to keep your mouth shut do you," Marique knew I was incapable, he was just making a statement.

"Stay back, Mar."

The one with tattoos of swastikas that looked like pinwheels over his eyes as he moved spoke with a gruff voice, the gruff voice acquired from hard drugs and inhaling cigarette smoke, "This world ain't meant for them, they should've stayed in the bushes where they belong." Losing my temper, I started to walk closer to the three.

"Old man, you don't have to die," said the one with a swastika on his chest, he was overweight, and had bigger breasts than some girls I had run into at the bar.

"Neither do you, racists." I clenched my fists and was ready to swing, all three had shivs, pulled out of their asses as far as I could tell.

This was about to get interesting.

"Watch out!" Marique yelled, a bar of yellow soap flew past my face and smacked one in the eye. I connected with a fist and broke his nose, took a shiv in the leg, it was a toothbrush filed down on cement and hopefully not packing hepatitis. It caught me by surprise, I fell over, he came stabbing at me with the heel of his foot, I took a few blows in the gut, reached up and punched him in the groin, buying myself ample time to stand. He rushed at me in rage, we locked, I landed a solid chop on his throat with a deft swipe and collapsed his windpipe, he tried to fight for his life, but died on the ground shortly after fighting for air. His eyelids shut and the swastika tattoos were going to deteriorate along with the rest of his body in due time.

"You could've joined us," the throat-tattooed guy said as he tried to stab me in the ribs. I grabbed and snapped his arm at the elbow, bones shot out, held onto his arm for a moment, it was my turn to speak.

"We supply the prison with goods and you are stupid enough to bite the hand that feeds," I said disappointed as I broke his leg with a kick at the knee, it crunched like a candy bar, the noise from water hitting tile floor washed out his screams. Another bar of soap flew past my face and hit big boy square in the testicles, to my surprise he did not freeze or stoop, big boy's sack must be made of Kevlar. He was coming at me with an improvised knife; crystal clear glass shard that had leather wrapped and fastened with a string for a handle.

"Walk away. I won't tolerate you boys calling my friend names." The words went past him as if he did not speak English, as if he did not know ethically right from wrong. I would teach him a lesson his mamma never taught him.

"You speak too much, shut up and let's settle this."

The two of us started to circle, his gang members were helplessly laying on the slick tile floor.

"Watch out, Hank!" Marique yelled, good friends do.

Big boy lunged, jolting his shiv at my throat, I stepped to the side, he was quick for his size and deceiving. The most skilled of the three, I discerned that his life must've been rough, he was wicked good with a knife. Slashing me across the arm, as I evaded, I bit my lip, when glass cuts you open, it hurts, the pain is excruciating. The ache lasts, where as if you were cut from a sharp knife, for instance, the pain is instantaneous and then gone. Blood mixed with water on the floor, I was annoyed at this, cutting me was not allowed. "You fucked with the wrong old man!" I yelled, if the guards came running, I would not be surprised.

"Careful, Hank!" My friend's voice echoed.

Taking a step forward, I put my bare foot on the ground, center of his feet, drove an elbow into his chin and bear-pawed him in the chest. Staggering back, big boy forced in a breath of air. Looking at me with curiosity, he said, "You know what you are doing, join us and we can free the world of their kind," he tilted his head to indicate Marique was who he had been talking about, "wipe out blacks one at a time!"

"Not in my life, I won't tolerate your prejudices."

"Fine, old man, I will take your life, then his," he spat on the ground to add to the bacteria and whatever else may have been crawling these poorly cleaned showers.

"Age is just a number, your parents ever tell you that?"

"Parents?" When he asked that I felt sad, not being properly raised could have pertained to why he developed into a skinhead.

"I'm tired of talking to you, worthless rat. Let's finish this before Marique smacks your big titties and puts you in the ICU, a black man kicking your ass with one arm. I am sure your gang would abrogate your sorry ass."

"Too much talking, right." He came back at me, a middle-aged man with a beard and bulbous figure. With a shiv walking out ahead of him, I grew cautious, very cautious, I did however kick the guy on the ground on his compound-fractured arm. Big boy went for stabs, at about six foot six, his reach far exceeded mine, I dodged another at the ribs, one at the eye, sucker punching him in the gut and then boxing his ears, he looked at me dazed. Sprinting at me, his next move telegraphed, I took a cheap shot and kneed him in the balls as I jabbed two fingers in his eyes.

"My eyes! What the bloody hell!" He stepped back as I kicked the knife from his hand.

"There is more of that where that came from." I smacked him on the side of his head with a closed fist like a rolled up newspaper and he, a bad dog. I hit him again and again until he launched and tackled me to the floor. Slick like there was oil, I slipped out of his grasp and grabbed him by the back of the head with a handful of skin.

"STOP! STOP!" he yelled, each crushing smack against the tile floor sending him closer and closer to the ICU, I would not kill him. Making him a vegetable might fix his prejudices. Blood splattered the ground around as I squished the big guy's face like stepping on a pile of dog shit.

"Hank, Hank, enough, enough, he is done, out, perhaps dead," said Marique.

"Yeah, well, ah, hell. I could use a drink." Marique gave me an arm and got me to my feet.

"Thanks, Hank, I would be dead if it were not for you."

"You say that a lot, you know that."

"Accept a thank you once in a while, it will build your character, you dusty bastard."

"What are you talking about, dusty?"

"Lack of better word, antiquated." He added, "Hard-ass."

"Flattering," I said, "too kind."

Shaking his head at me, "Get some clothes on, you've been fighting naked, the fags catch notice out there, they may ask for a lesson."

"Suddenly, I have worse nightmares. I don't have a problem with Gerard or Joe, even Patrick for that matter, if it makes them gay they can sleep with other men," I was washing off in the shower, contaminated floor and all, "just don't come trying to tie me down or get in my pants. Friends, that's fine, you know me, I am the least judgmental."

"Yes you are."

"You have to pee?"

"Why, you thirsty?"

"Quit the shit, Marique, no, the skinhead there with a broken arm and busted up leg needs his wounds sanitized."

Catching my drift, Marique walked over and pissed on the guy who had threatened his life, the man screamed as bad as when I broke the bones (poetic justice). We walked out of the bathroom, I told Kurwack what had happened and gave him a speedball to take care of everything and keep me out of the warden's office. Nobody saw what happened besides my friend and I, therefore nobody else had to know. Although things may change from here out, the leniency, being unattended to the bathrooms, our privileges weighed and considered more closely.

29

"Where did you learn how to fight like that, you have to have had some practice?" Marique asked as we sat in the stands near the track out in the yard.

"My brother, older brother. He was a nut, could fight at tournaments for karate and win first place almost every time, he boxed too, that was his passion. He trained me up until his death."

"Sad, sad story, I wish I could have met your brother if he was a lot like you."

"He was, though we had different temperaments than one another." A tear stuck in the crook of my eye, "Miss him, you know."

"Yeah, I miss my son, and I miss my wife."

"Your wife, you never mentioned her before, what was she like, Marique?"

"You keep your filthy comments about women away from her name, okay."

"Okay, you know I am a gentleman, I would not do such a thing, not about her."

"Good," he grabbed a cigarette from my pack, had me light it, I lit mine and smoked as we spoke. "She had big eyelashes, round cheeks, creamy mocha skin with curly hair that moved like springs as she walked. Her name was Amy, my wife always wore dresses that covered her ankles, real proper woman like the old west." I nodded. "Her laugh was addictive like nicotine, being separated from Amy to this day still has me handling imperishable withdrawals.

"She laughed at birds that chirped outside, she laughed at my son when he belched or ran faster than her, she laughed at me while I kissed her neck and made marks. Amy was intelligent, she could pass any test, she knew every word. Her voice was high pitched, not too high where it is annoying, but high enough you fall in love with the sound of it. Have you heard a voice like that, Hank?"

"Yes, yes, of course, girl I knew way back when, her voice was that sort as you described, Marique. Tell me more, please."

"Amy ran for governor of Illinois one year, she was not selected because she was black and a woman most surely. She made a living as a teller at a bank."

"Hey, my wife too," I interjected.

"Amy was a beautiful woman, the world was a voluptuous place with her in it."

"She died, what from?"

"My wife was going through labor with our second child, they both died on the operating table."

"I, I am sorry to hear that … Life is … a tragedy."

"Oh, don't I know that. You have kids that are alive, Hank, don't forget that. They may not write, but they know, know who you are and that you are alive."

"Very true, I would like to reconnect with them, when I get out of here, that is."

"Soon enough, just try not to kill anyone else. Frankly, I am not sure how many bodies is Kurwack's limit before he has the warden reprimand your ass and throw you in solitary for a month."

"You think I'd get a month?"

"Month in solitary, an extra four years at least added to your sentence."

"I remember when I only used that word 'sentence' when referring to lines and phrases in a book. As a writer, I hate that word now, ironically."

"You write well, you write with soul."

I lit another cigarette and enjoyed it, after dodging death again and saving my friend, nothing to complain about there.

"And spirit too, get me some brandy and I can show you how well I do, indeed."

"I know you're not lying, I've seen it before. People ask about poets, you know?"

"Ask what?"

"When they speak, hear you answer–why do you not speak poetry out loud off the top of your head?"

"It just doesn't work that way, Marique, people asked me that back in the day, after I mentioned that I write poems, either that or they ask if I am a sissy. Humans aren't wired that way, at least I'm not, I write poems, I do not speak them unless I reiterate what I have already written."

"Spoken like a man who knows his art. Women, men, they do not understand, we are human. I get that, misunderstood. Before you smoke your whole entire pack and want to head in, would you like to play a game of chess, Hank?"

"Only if you are going to actually try to win this time." I gave him another cigarette and we smoked together like we normally do.

"If you quit being an ass and reading ten moves ahead, maybe I will."

"Can't promise anything. It is natural, I am teaching, if anything."

"And I am learning."

30

A couple weeks went by and Luis came to visit, not much had transpired since. In prison there is only so much to do, and I, I am living it like a king in comparison to most, along with my friend Marique. No skinheads have bothered us in the showers since, Kurwack still comes by for a speedball, like any consistent addict, Kowski brings me books with parcels to slip under the bars of my cell. I have been reading a lot of fiction lately, I try to read at minimum a book a week, and write for four hours a day, whether that be poetry or short stories.

The days of the week sometimes fly by, that or the fact I forget to mark a calendar contributes to why I never remember the day of the week. Our warden here, Mr. Jan, as he is formally known, switched the roles for the convicts, Marique was moved to do custodial work, he complains night and day about the fact that it is near impossible to mop with one arm. Mar is not the strongest fellow, his arm is thin as a rail, handling a mop sodden with water that weighted it down would be an arduous task. His favorite part about his job is cleaning Jan's office, he reads through the papers on the desk to gain intel and, after finding the key for the drawers, he found a stash of filthy, vintage adult magazines, a handgun, and photographs of little boys. Sick to my stomach at the thought, I could foresee that, however. Jan was five-six and diabetic, he had a tendency to do strip searches, and worked as a priest on the weekends at an old metal-roofed church down near the main strip in Aumsville.

Jan, the rotten son of a bitch, moved me from tending the yard to down near the boiler, where all of the washing machines and dryers are. With as many men as we have here, I am washing clothes and sheets around the clock, my hands shrivel and turn to prunes. The sheets from inmates' beds are repulsive, stained with semen from lack of action with any woman, brown stains from those who ran out of toilet paper, yellow spots from men who were not potty-trained clearly. I hate my job, I really do. The rotation will come as soon as Jan feels there is a need, apparently the white supremacists were partnered in areas with the blacks and Mexicans, which subsequently resulted in two deaths and they were not the supremacists, unfortunately.

Today was the day my oldest friend came by to visit, older than Marique–having a few good friends can make life worth living. I walked up to the glass partitions that separated visitors from the freedom-deprived prisoners; eight booths with phones crudely placed on the particle board barrier laminated with false wood grain that separated a convict from the next to give a sense of privacy; chairs with four legs and a leather back that was torn sat at each booth. Out of eight booths, two were vacant.

Sitting down, I was chained to the floor by my ankles and my hands were given two feet of leeway with the chain on the platform in front. Luis was on the other side of the glass, he looks older each time he drops by, a job like his will do that to you. Reaching for the phone, we both held eye contact, our facial expressions said all of the words that needed to be said. You can read a great deal by looking at a person's face, knowing Luis as long as I have, it was second nature.

Placing the scratched and clawed phone to my ear, I spoke to my buddy, "Hey, you look like hell."

"That is easy for you to say, you are in it," his saddened eyes made me feel the pity he portrayed.

"Hell is all around us, depends on what you make of it. I know my life has not been easy, you know that well. You were a deputy when Abe and Josiah were killed and I murdered an affiliate of Larson's gang. That was close to hell, killing my wife was along those lines, living here is selfish. I do not have to man up to my children, I do not have to see their faces as I try and explain."

"Perhaps one day, Hank. How are they treating you here?"

"The usual, laid back, for the most part, as long as I keep my nose to the grindstone, they get free labor out of me. Warden can't complain about that, I have been doing good as I can, if you know what I mean, Luis."

"Certainly, I miss having a drink with you, we are old-timers now. We are supposed to live the Faulkner lifestyle in a big house and drink expensive whiskey."

"You know I'd trade a lot for that, getting out of here right now to chase some tail and drink ambrosia. I've been wanting to play a game of pool for quite a while now."

"Hank, I am sorry to say, but there is no way you'd come close to beating me."

"Why do you say that, have you been practicing without me?"

"Had to catch up, your skill was far more formidable than mine. Now I can put old English on the ball like Minnesota Fats."

"Think of my sentence as a blessing, pal, the fact I have been locked up so long has given you the time to hone your skill. When I get out, we might just go have a game at the pub there in Carlton."

"It's under a new owner now."

"Yeah, still the same inside and out?"

"Mostly, the scoundrel that bought the place raised the prices on everything, including the jukebox and the billiards. You know how we used to play for free on Sundays?"

"As long as we were buying drinks."

"Right, well the new owner decided that that had to be thrown out the door, along with all the people that worked there."

"What a bastard, that is too bad. Huh, what else has changed? We are usually so busy talking about me inside here and my treatment, I have not heard the juicy details about out there."

"Remember, we are on a clock here, I do have some items I would like to discuss with you a little later."

"Fair enough, so what's been going on?"

Luis looked at me, spooked, knowing the reaction I may already have to what he would say. "Alright, you know the lake you liked to go fishing at as a kid, the one you always talked about taking a boat out in and jumping off to swim in, the lake that hangs off the bridge right there in Carlton?"

"You're scaring me, what, what?" I cracked my knuckles as a nervous twitch of a kind, felt good to crack something when adrenaline runs rampant. Little things can get to me, I try not to allow it to happen, sad to say that is just the way it is.

"The city decided to drain the lake," Luis closed his eyes, abashed, "the dam was getting up there in age and cracking, it would've flooded the lower park and the fields for miles around. Sorry, Hank."

"Permanently?"

"Afraid so, a family of farmers bought the land and have harvested twice already. They are not giving up their land for the life of them."

"Which family purchased my lake?"

"The Brunders."

"Them? I know them. I went to school with the son and daughter of Phil and Margaret Brunder."

"Phil and Margaret are deceased."

"Happened a while back, right?"

"Yeah, late fall one year. Phil passed and Margaret drank the hemlock–Romeo and Juliet fans, must be."

"Must be."

Peering through the glass at me as if he were deciding if I were actually real, Luis started to mention one of my babies, "Your coupe's running strong."

"You've been taking care of it like I told you, Luis?" I was upset as any boy who had to watch his crush be kissed by another man.

"Yup, spit shine the rims like Willy down on Main Street shines my boots. Change the oil regularly and wax it every other month. You can have it back when you are released."

"No, no, I want you to enjoy it."

"You sure?"

"Ah... you know me, man, I don't mind her being used, but I miss her. That car and I had some wild escapades cruising the Pacific and storming through the streets in Portland at night."

"The keys are always yours to take back, when you get out, I will return them, promise, you're going to need a car, Hank, since you had me get rid of Maybelline's truck."

"Luis, don't worry about it for now. I still have nearly ten years left here. Long years I intend to survive."

"You better."

"How's the house, you've been maintaining it for me as well?"

"Definitely, listen, Hank, you don't have to pay me anything." With my parents death and my inheritance, I have enough money I can pay Luis a pittance each time he goes and works on the place down Old Mac, not to mention all of the reconnaissance he does for me with my children.

"Hey, it's nothing, alright. I should be paying you more," gesticulating with my hands and yanking on the chains that bound me.

"They should do away with this glass barrier and have it where we can sit in a room together. You're not violent unless provoked, same as any man. This is the only prison in the state that does that too, if I had more authority I would do something about it." That was Luis's way of saying if he had the time, he would, he had enough weight he could move around and try to better this joint with, with enough ambition.

"Most inmates' families don't come back for a second visit. It's too hard to just look through a sheet of glass, like watching your loved one on TV and not being allowed to touch. Damn hard, damn hard it is."

"You're telling me, Hank. I am out here a free man and my best friend is stuck behind bars 365 days a year."

"We are all circumscribed, finite, caged by society. To be truly free is to break the law. Land of the free, this country. As free as it gets as a unit, go off on your own and isolate yourself, strip away your existence. That in turn is the most palpable freedom one can attain."

"In some ways, I think you're right," he said hesitantly, as an officer of the law and all.

"How's being chief treating you, still running around and chasing the mamacitas with your baton?"

"That is classified information, you do not reach the requirements to attain such pertinent files," Luis spoke like a robot and I only laughed.

"Question confirmed. What about deputy Cleveland?"

"Still worthless as a perished food item in a five-star kitchen. He crashed his cruiser last week chasing down a kid on a bike. How, how is that even possible? I do not even want to know the answer, his stupidity eludes me."

"Figures, why was he chasing the kid down?" I scrunch my forehead, wondering.

"Wasn't riding in a straight enough line, apparently."

Sounds pathetic, petty if you ask me. "That's all. Is that even against the law?"

"No, but he thinks it should be. The kid ended up having an ounce of marijuana in his jacket pocket."

"Did the kid get charged?"

"No, Cleveland forgot to read the kid his rights."

"Small town cops, they get the bad rep for people like Cleveland."

"No kidding, if he was smarter than a rock, we might actually get some credit when credit is due." Luis rubbed his eyeballs with the palm of his light brown hands.

"You can only expect so much, Luis, the less you would expect, the less you would be disappointed."

"Speaking of the bar earlier."

"Luis, stop."

"But, Hank."

"Listen, you do not have to apologize."

"I feel responsible in a way."

"Friends do that. It was no way, shape or form your fault I went to Portland that night, and May ... just drop it."

"Only if we would have stayed there longer at the pub, perhaps you would not be locked behind bars."

"Halt dwelling on the things you cannot change, that will drive a man crazy. Have you been drinking a lot lately?"

"Eh, you know me. Bottle of whiskey a week."

"That all?"

"Depends on the week."

"Sounds about right–hey, hold on one minute." I hooked the phone up and turned to look at the guard who opened the door, he was telling us that we had ten minutes left. "We have ten minutes left."

"Time flies, partner."

"That it does."

"I have something to show you, I waited till the end to let you know." Luis put an envelope out on the counter in front of him and pulled out a baker's dozen of photographs. "Your boy, James, he had something come up, decided to take a few pictures."

My heartbeat rose, pounding, I got excited when he talked about my sons. "What came up, is he alright, healthy? Ain't drinking like his old man? Come on, show me."

Photos placed against the tempered glass, "He had twins, and is due for another one in a few months."

I cried as bad as I did when Maybelline died, tears of joy in this state of affairs, two baby girls. Two beautiful baby girls that had eyes the color of bottled glass as their grandmother's were. So cute, tiny, lovable. They were precious. I still remember holding my boys. No words could explain the true sensation of holding "your" child for the first time, a million words and questions run through your head.

"Girls, twins. Holy shit, Luis, does that mean I am a grandpa?"

"Yes, you are, Hank. Grandfather."

"I, I wish to meet them. There is so much I am missing out on," I grabbed a cigarette and started to smoke from nerves, "in this labyrinth."

"Trust me, I know, there is so much we are missing out on."

"Did you catch their names?"

"No, I was at a distance when I took these pictures. I just keep tabs on them."

"Thanks, I could never repay you for all that you do, buddy."

"Don't mention it, grandpa."

The voice of the guard came loud like thunder, "All rise, time's up boys. Back to your cells."

"Luis, you take care now. I want to see you when I get out of here, alright?"

"You too, I'll see you again as soon as I can!"

We both hung up, and walked our separate ways.

31

Sixty-three years old, damn. Did I ever think I would make it to such a ripe old age, no.

I did, I survived the treacherous years inside. Now was the time to be freed, twenty-five years of my life eroded behind bars. Locked away with time being the only key. Time came to open my cell. Time came to set me free. Marique was balling like a baby, I knew he would be fine, a couple of the other guys said they would protect him for me.

"Last day, old man," Marique said, eyes swollen, despising the phrase that escaped his mouth.

"That it is, it's been a long time, my friend," I blinked rapidly, waiting for a day for twenty-five years and having it finally come around the bend can throw your whole system into a wild, manic state.

"That it has, you going to miss me?"

"More than ever, I have enough stories to last me a lifetime."

"No more playing chess, not for some time, until I get released."

"I am afraid I will be dead and in the dirt before they let you out, Marique."

"Don't say that, leave me some hope, old man."

"Business will be hard to handle by yourself, pick wisely who you cut in."

He pushed his glasses back to reveal the tiger that lurked within, "Give me a hug, my friend, I know the one arm makes it awkward, but, nonetheless, it has to be done." We hugged like men and cried like this was the end, in a way it was.

"Marique, you want a cigarette for old times sake?"

"Last one you'll ever offer me, sure." I put it in his mouth and lit it, we were standing in our cell facing one another.

"A memento, here."

"Hank, I can't take this." I handed him my reusable lighter from the railroad days decades ago.

"You need something to hold onto, I know it may be hard to use with one arm, but you can improvise. Take and swipe the wheel against your pant leg and it should strike the flint. You have to do it quickly, like so," I demonstrated, he tried and had it down in a few attempts.

"You've taught me more than my own parents, Hank."

"That some kind of joke, you don't even know your parents." He choked on cigarette smoke, always and forever a wiseass.

"You catch on quick. I have been listening to your wisecracks for twenty-five years, Marique, a youngster could tell you're full of shit." I patted him on the shoulder, took a deep drag and exhaled.

"Don't forget to wipe your ass so you don't smell like a bum."

"And you, don't forget to polish your silver-capped teeth, buddy."

"Kurwack is going to miss waking you up in the morning."

"I can live without that, as far as a junkie goes, he can be a handful."

"Kowski is going to miss dropping off literature for you to read."

"I know, he will miss the tip I gave him too. Make sure to play chess every day, maybe one day you will get the chance to beat me."

"Twenty-five years, Hank, and I have not prevailed in a single match against you. I am either extremely bad or you are just that good."

"A fanatic. I can play. With you to play against, I've become a practitioner, so have you. You may not be able to triumph over me, but other guys in here will crumble before you. Trust me, you're not bad at all."

"Thanks, you want a glass of whiskey before you go? Kurwack should be coming to get you any minute."

"Yeah, why the hell not, make it a triple shot and refrain from spitting in it this time."

"That is why you say it tastes unique, gives it flavor."

"You know that's a load of crap."

Marique made our drinks and I smoked another cigarette, the liquor went down smooth, I spoke of many things with my friend for the last time behind bars. I moved my pipe for opium to inside his pillow case so that he did not have difficulty getting to it. Friends, without them I may not have made it this long, this far. Sixty-three years old, I still can't fathom the notion of my existence to this day. As humans, we make a lot of turns, I twisted and turned, rode high in April and shot down in May. I did not take the easy route, most of it was not my choice, fate has a funny way of sticking it to you.

"You are already up and drinking, you drunk," Kurwack mused, glowering.

"You are still as dumb as ever. Let me out of this cage, you bastard." Our morning routine, as per usual, I would not have it any other way.

"Whoa, whoa, grandpa, keep it down, you'll have a heart attack." He punched his chest and started faking convulsions, if that were the way I died, I could at least say that it was fitter than most.

"Not today. Today's the day I leave. Let me out, before I grab you by your gizzard and smack you around a bit."

"Marique and you been in there drinking all morning, I can smell it from here." He rattled his nightstick on our cell bars.

"Yeah, and you have been doing cocaine all morning."

"How can you tell?"

"You are notorious for leaving it on your nose."

"Oh. Make me a drink."

Marique chimed in, "What the hell you mean 'make me a drink' I ain't your lackey."

"Yeah, but you got alcohol out and in sight at 8 a.m. Let me get a swig."

"Let me the hell out of here, Kurwack, you son of a bitch," I said.

"Don't talk about my mother like that."

"Why? She deserves the title and you are too embarrassed to accept."

"Just pass me a bottle and let me take the edge off."

"Alright, just this once," Marique relented.

"Damn straight," Kurwack, proud of his small achievement.

"First thing I do when I get out of here is to send you a bag of dog shit once a week to your house as long as I live." Kurwack straightened, looked at me knowing full well I meant it.

"You better not, Hank, I will smack the shit out of Marique if you do."

"What the hell you gotta bring me in on this one for, Kurwack," Marique regretted handing him the bottle now.

"Touch Marique and I will burn your house down, blow up your car, and tie cinder blocks to your legs, then toss you into the Willamette," I said.

"Sounds like a threat," Kurwack glared at me.

"I could kill you now where you stand. I am an old man, no wife, I do not have much to lose," I said dispassionately.

"Just don't send the dog crap in the mail. I am allergic to dogs," Kurwack was squeamish at the thought.

"What a wuss, right, Hank," Marique slapped me on the shoulder with his good arm.

"Quit nursing that bottle, you big baby, hand it back to Marique and let me out," I was impatient, eager to set my sail.

"I guess it's that time." Kurwack unlocked my cage and walked me out; I turned to say my goodbye to my friend of twenty-five years. One of the best men I'd ever known.

"Godspeed, Marique, I love you like a brother," tears dripped down my face and onto my prison attire.

"That is because we are brothers. Take it easy, old friend." It doesn't matter who your parents are, you can bond with anyone given the chance.

I hugged him and walked away, never to turn back again. The inmates screamed and hollered as Marique signaled them that today was my last day here. Like apes at the zoo, they made noises and threw items, arms reached out through bars to grab and shake, pat and slap, I was in some ways going to miss this place. Miss this life. But, I knew good things don't last forever, neither do the bad. As humans, we are only temporary, nothing is evermore.

32

All of the stories and movies at drive-ins out near the countryside with high class projectors that play prison movies, they play films that try to attest for prison life. Subjectively, I would say the most emotional part is when a convict gets to walk away free. Leaving prison was a relief, inside those walls was traumatizing, I made the best of it as I could. Damn sure I did. In movies, they like to show how when prisoners are finally released, the ex-inmate is dressed in his finest Sunday clothes, not iron-slicked slacks worn down past repair. Jan threw my clothes away, surely he thought I would die before I was released. I ended up making out with slacks that were far too long and far too gone, the waste was right and tight and the pockets were covered with sawdust like whoever wore these before apparently worked with wood. The shirt they gave me had a few holes from cigarette burns, a gash to one side with either ketch-up or blood staining it, I hope not the latter. Least appealing aspect was the color: yellow.

I skipped and smoked a cigarette, when it was an occasion for a fine Cuban cigar like my daddy had smoked. With nothing on me besides hide and clothes, I burned under the heat of a warm July day. A breeze blew that rippled my shirt, air graced my presence as I walked through the final gate, a free man. Luis was waiting outside with my coupe and scooted out the driver's side to clasp me with hands, a hug for the first time in more than two decades.

"You are thin as a rail, Hank."

"That is all you have to say, quit squeezing like a ninny."

He looked at me, took a step back and twisted his neck to the side, tilting his head down, squinting one eye and biting a lip while simultaneously raising a wrinkly finger to point at me, "What the hell are you wearing, looks like the clothes we strip off the dead before sending them to the morgue."

"Fuck, those are probably nicer than what I am wearing."

"Startling, no way you are catching any action in them."

"Don't sell me short, I may be old, but I can still get it up."

"Sixty-three, wily old duffer," he rocked his head back and forth, astonished.

"You look better from on the other side of the glass, Luis."

"Bastard, you were probably high on narcotics at the time, that is why."

"Shit, can't argue with that."

"You driving or am I?" He asked a rhetorical question, knowing full well what the answer was to be.

"Do you even have to ask that question?"

"No," he had a pie-eating grin.

"Toss me the keys," I caught them mid-air, "Thanks, let's get the hell out of here and never come back."

"Amen."

I sat back down in my coupe, bucket seats just like I remembered them, interior spotless, mirrors wiped free of dust and chrome glaring into my eye. Luis retrofitted a stereo, and added a pair of fuzzy dice dangled like cow balls in my face, and sunglasses with black rims and gold flakes were fit snugly next to the E-brake. "You shouldn't have."

"What?"

"The glasses, I have always wanted a pair like this."

"I know, turn the stereo on, Hank." I did, classic jazz embraced my eardrums and could be felt down in my gut.

"Luis, you are too sweet. I have been listening to Johnny Cash every day since I can remember when."

"His songs are an epidemic spread throughout the stations, can't seem to escape "Ring Of Fire" like the plague."

"What is this?"

"The fuzzy dice? I thought you would like those as a nice addition."

"No, no those are fine. This?" I pointed at some halfway dressed woman figurine with flowers around her neck and suction-cupped to my dash.

"Oh that, that is a bobblehead of a hula dancer."

"I have not seen a woman's behind up close and personal in too damn long, this is the best you could do?" Pretending to be upset, I cast my eyes down at the steering wheel, took one hand and shifted the car into first and took off.

"Well, it is not like prostitutes are legal, and you are too kind to deal with a whore."

"True. I got a feeling we are going to have fun, you know what I have in mind?"

"What might that be, Hank?"

"Guess."

"Strip club and drinks, we are celebrating aren't we?"

"You bet your brown ass, we are. Did you bring me money like I planned last time you visited, a couple packs of smokes too?"

"Yeah, right here." He reached into the glove box and pulled out two packs of filtered cigarettes, "You want a cig now?"

"Yeah toss me one." He did, "You have a lighter?" He did, "Thanks, need to buy a new one, gave my old trusty one to Marique."

"Marique needed more than a lighter, Hank."

"I know, I gave him the best I could, left him a poem underneath his bed sheet."

"How did it go?"

I read it to him off the top of my head. Marique was possibly reading it himself right now, after trying to lay back down for a nap, I got him fairly drunk before I left, handed him all my rations to eat. He is sitting with a full stomach, drunk on memories, as he reads my poem.

-Dear Marique

Best of friends,
beat down by the able folk of our time
tricked to yard work and sad night
played with, like a game of Russian roulette.

The wind will bring a smell of tobacco smoke
the sea will breathe a salty breath
my house will be empty, but a home
the cell we shared bonded and loaned.

I am sorry I had to go,
together we were better off than alone
at distance now, call on the telephone
bring your smile and one arm
to the pearly gates above,
again one day
we too will be at home.

"That is really sweet, Hank." I think I saw a tear come to his eye, Luis lit a cigarette and blew smoke out the cracked window. As if the words bore too much weight, crushing under the impact, I could see him strong-willed, holding his composure steady. His mind raced as he chased scenery to assuage the sadness boring down.

"Thanks, buddy," grasping the wheel, I unstrained arthritis-aching hands. I'd miss Marique, damn, I really would.

"Will you write me one, one day when I die?" A droplet still loitered in his eye.

"Hopefully that day will never come."

For an old man I have experienced plenty of death, to this day none of it sits well. Live a long hearty life and I do not agonize over demise, perish far before expiration and I suffer, the wrath of one's appressed to my soul haunt me in dreams forevermore.

"What do you mean?" He did not know, know what I know. Luis and I have lived contrastive lives, how could he feel it deep down as I do.

"What I mean is, I am relying on natural selection to pick me off before you, that way I do not have to write that poem," selfish words flowing out with a bite, demeanor deceptive in account.

"Narcissistic bastard."

"That is comme il faut," I think I have earned it, if ever there was a thing to earn.

"What?"

"I said that is comme il faut."

"There you go again," he said. Luis tugged on the neck of his shirt, "I saved some news for you."

Dammit, "What?"

"I sent your poetry you have been writing the last twenty-five years to Portland to get edited and they want to publish it."

"You," I lost my breath, "you have to be kidding me."

"No, not at all," he said, pleased with himself.

"That, that's terrific! Astounding!" At such a decrepit age, I marveled at the effect of exhilaration like a diminutive toddler.

"They're using your material, Hank!"

"I'm shocked."

"Your work has soul, there is no negating that."

"I owe you, Luis."

"Nothing."

"No, I do."

"If you insist, pay me back in the afterlife. I have all I need now that you are on the loose." Conflicting emotions had my eyes wet, Luis sat there stock-still, showing teeth. "We have to run an errand first before we can go to a clip joint."

"What might that be?"

"Just follow my directions and turn when I tell you to turn, dammit, I won't lead you astray, partner." Most honest guy I know, the teacher told me as a lad that Abraham Lincoln never told a lie, if Abe was still standing today, I'd say he would be the one emulating Luis.

I followed his directions to the point, our destination was downtown Salem, where a shop made tailored suits, fine quality, Luis had heard. Likely we would substitute the tailored suit for what fit best, given the time constraints. The storefront was emblazoned with gold and silver paint that wrapped around in a Czecholslovakian Coat Of Arms lion adorned with its golden crown. Squares of cement were freshly put into place for the sidewalk leading to the threshold, I parked the coupe and spit on the ground at a meter that made me pay an outrageous amount to park. Times had changed indeed.

"Why are we here, Luis?"

"What do you think, to get you a tailor-made suit."

"No, no, that won't be necessary. That would take too long, a normal suit off the rack would suffice."

"You are dressed as ill as the bums under the bridge, but I accept the compromise."

"You did not have to put it so crudely, my friend."

"Honesty, Hank, friends, that is what we are for."

"Don't I know it."

Stopping by the facade, we started to smoke cigarettes like bad boys, I took a healthy drag until a quarter inch of ash dropped to the ground. Luis liked to take it slow, he said the women he had been with liked that about him, slow. I live too fast at times, inadvertently, to know full well what he means.

"After you," I said, holding a brass door handle and shutting the squeaky door behind me gently as not to wake the tailor napping on the job. Business was slow apparently, either that or he had insomnia and when he could sleep, he did.

"This is my first time here, Hank, try not to scare the gentlemen." Walking through the store, there were suits premade and ties, mannequins, dress shirts on racks and cufflinks with watches under the glass for security purposes.

"I am abashed, my dear friend, you think just because I have spent twenty-five years in the slammer that I am a 'scary' guy. For your information, I am an amiable fellow, do not forget that latter when I beat your behind at pool." Luis made a hush-up noise for me to keep my voice down as we lurked through the store up to the front desk without waking my new tailor.

Luis, turning back to make a gesture with his hands as if to convey his message, "It's not because specifically you were in a cell for so long, it is your eyes, Hank. A man who has been through what you have has a certain look in their eyes. Inherently, most men and women can read that without even meaning to." Eyes, hmm … his voice was sincere, I do believe it to be true. After you kill a man or two, three or four, five, maybe six, you start to lose count when you are just trying to simplistically survive. You can take the convict out of prison, but you cannot take the prison out of the convict. Luis was right, my eyes are a great deal darker than they used to be, the cordial blue as glacier eyes I had possessed transmuted into a hollow dark blue like the depths of the Pacific, hard and pressed with a chill that bites at those willing to gander.

"I can respect that, regard this: death is in everyone's eyes, even if they don't know it yet, pal." I stepped forward to slap him on the back.

"Quiet now, let me wake sleeping beauty," Luis said, dropping the subject.

Clearing his throat did not awake the tailor. Auburn hair was cascading his face, a younger boy, about thirty, I would say. Sleeping on the job was a pet peeve of Luis's, his deputy Cleveland was doing it day-after-day. Smacking one hand down on the counter and reading the name tag on the boys shirt, "Good day, Erick, my partner here would like to have a suit fitted."

"Ah, you startled me, friend," Erick's mannerisms were delayed, slow, uninterested. His voice soft like a petal plucked from a rose. "What brings you in here, ah, that is right, you said a suit, does your friend want it tailored or would he like a cheaper one that fits nice enough?"

"I said tailored if that is not too much trouble, appears you were busy counting sheep. I hope my partner and I are not bothering you," Luis told the man with dissatisfaction in his tone.

I spoke to Luis in private, yanking him by the shoulder and bringing him around the clothes rack, "Buddy, I do not need a tailored suit, sure it is fine, but unnecessary. As Erick said, one that fits 'nice enough' would fit the purpose just fine."

"But, Hank, no, no, I want to buy you a nice suit for tonight."

"One that is not tailored will do just fine, if it is a matter of money?"

"No, not money at all, I have been saving for this day for quite some time—didn't even sleep a wink last night."

"Neither did I, even the opium did not put me to rest."

"What? You started doing that junk?"

"It helps, kills my nightmares to a degree. Look, let us talk about that tonight or another time, if you do not mind. I hate to make the gentleman wait while we bicker over here like a married couple."

"You wish I would put a ring on your homely finger?" My lip quivered slightly at the mention of my finger. "Tailored suit, alright, do not want it any other way."

"Luis, just buy me a nice watch and cufflinks, it will save you some coin and allow me to tell time. And, the cufflinks will go nicely."

"Cufflinks come with the suit regardless."

"Damn, I saw a fedora back there that I liked on the wall, that will suffice then if you have a hole in your pocket where money is burning through."

"Deal."

Erick stood there and directed me to a pair of slacks, I told him that I wanted black, slim fit and debonair. They came with a petite coin pocket, smooth as silk, classy button and an invincible zipper, as Erick informed me. Luis decided we were going to match tonight like lovers, I gave him a sideways glance and said the hell with it. Next, I was handed a white dress shirt, hand-stitched and made of premium quality cotton, had a split yoke, removable collar stays, mother of pearl buttons that gleamed, reinforced seams and hand-sewn cuffs. The tie I grabbed was black with two different shades that were angled diagonally and rotated every other in an eye-pleasing striped pattern.

"You would not happen to have any dress shoes, would you?" I asked Erick.

"No, no, I do not."

"Give him yours, I will pay you handsomely," Luis was about to start negotiating.

"How much?" Erick looked from his black dress shoes with double-nickel buckles back to me and asked, "What size do you wear anyhow?"

"Shoes such as those, nine and a half."

"These are nines."

"Let me try those suckers on first before Luis throws out a price, that fair, Erick?"

"Sure," he slipped off his shoes and kicked them over to me, I sat down on a stool, "bought them a month ago, just broke them in too." I tested his shoes out, it is weird wearing another man's shoes, today I have worn more than one. His were nicer than what I had on currently and fit like a glove.

"Wow, fit tight and feel just right."

"Forty bucks?" Luis threw out.

"Sixty."

"Fifty."

"Fifty-five."

"Fine," Luis handed Erick the money and I kept the shoes on, buckled, and tapped around as if I were a dancer.

"Cufflinks, that black fedora with a feather and a watch, Erick, chop chop, my buddy, I have things to catch up on," I said.

"Right over here," Erick led me to the glass case, Luis grabbed four or five fedoras and tried them on my head to see which fit and which didn't. "Take which you want, sir, I will ring it up." He removed a glass top and I grabbed the first that caught my eye. Silver cufflinks and a wind-up skeleton watch with Roman numerals made from real gold, its mechanism showed a shiny gold besides the gears and coil. Taking the leather strap and fitting it on, I wound up the wheel and set the time.

"Take these too, I will leave them with you while I go try this new suit on if that is all right, Erick."

"Certainly, let me show you the fitting room." A small room as large as my cell was had a bench to sit on and a mirror, I dressed, set the fedora on a hook at the back of the door, slacks slipped on, shirt, a blazer that was black I snagged on the way to the room and put my cufflinks on. Dropped my fedora on and re-buckled my shoes, I was ready to go and, damn, did I look good for an old-timer.

"Luis, what do you think?" I asked as I looked him over in a new suit and tie.

"Stunning, tie your tie a little tighter, Hank, looks like a slack noose."

"Look better now?"

"Yes, let's get the hell out of here and go to a club."

Erick accepted Luis's money, gave us each a rectangular plastic container with toothpicks stashed inside. I felt sharp as I walked out the door, cleansing my system of prison one step at a time. Luis looked over at me as he began to preen his blazer until it settled right. "What happened with your clothes that you wore in there?"

"Tossed them."

"Yeah, where?"

"Behind the counter as Erick restocked the racks."

"Trying to scare the poor feller, are you?"

"The way you made it sound, it was inevitable."

Luis rummaged inside his new pocket to pull out a cigarette for me and a copper flask. "Here, I figured you might be thirsty."

"Might, no, I unquestionably am." Taking a slug, I wiped my lips as we made our way back to the coupe with Luis in his suit, me in mine. His was a great deal easier to pick out since he matched mine with what was off the rack. They both fit nicely, like a glove.

33

Salem and strip clubs, clip joints, all the same idea. Rip-off, I walked through the front door with Luis to my right, there were a myriad of women, lounging men, drinks were placed on counters and tips were given. I felt out of my element after all these years; the first place I decided to go was to check the ass end of a stripper. Luis wanted to come see what was on the menu, he tossed down a dollar at the table, a fine black woman with curly blonde hair she must've dyed came over to snatch his dollar bill with a subtle swoop of her breasts. I laughed and started coughing at the same time, an awkward combination.

"She grabbed it better with her breast than you would with your teeth," I said with tears rolling down my cheeks.

"She has practice, toss some money down, you stingy bastard," Luis grabbed a dollar bill from my hand and set it down. Before the end of the song, she came over and picked up the bill, leaned forward to grab me by the chest and shove my face into her dollar-snatcher.

"There you go, Hank." It did not feel right, up until that moment being here felt fine, now, no. I had a sickness in my gut and ran to the bathroom to puke. Maybelline, after all these years I thought I would be over her.

Love, true love never dies. It is eternal.

Sitting back down next to Luis, he looked at me like he knew what was going on, "It's her, isn't it, Hank?"

"Yeah, yeah, it is. Let's go get a shot of whiskey to celebrate our prolonged reuniting, and a shot of tequila for my beloved."

"Alright, I figured as much might happen. Just wanted to show you a good time, partner."

"I know, you are doing a good job indeed. The night is still young, I haven't even made it back to my house yet."

"True, you want top-shelf?"

"Yeah, sure." He threw down a few dollars and we took our shots straight and neat, no coughing like nippers, and walked out the door.

"Cigarette?" I asked.

"Here, try to slow down, you don't want cancer." Luis passed me a smoke.

"We all have cancer," I said pressing my lips together and raising my eyebrows.

"Keep your philosophical shit to yourself, I just got you back, you ain't going to go dying on me just yet."

"Yet, perspective, maybe tomorrow?"

"Start driving." I did, turning the key in the ignition, the engine came to life and the exhaust hummed as I sped off back out into the street. It was getting dark, around ten if my new watch holds the time true.

"What's next?" Luis asked me, smoking a filtered cigarette down to the butt, flicked it out the window and started up another.

"You'd think in all this time I would have planned the day out better."

"Misbegotten is usually your style."

"Kiss my ass."

"Pass."

"That bar in McMinnville still around behind the dealership?"

"The one you used to work at?"

"Yeah, the Ford one, that bar still back there?"

"Should be."

After a fifty-minute drive we arrived, drinking off a bottle of whiskey Luis pulled out of the back seat, my buzz was long gone and I was drunk. I maneuvered my coupe around two cars and a full-size truck in the parking lot, found an empty spot, locked the doors, and dropped the key in an inner breast pocket that allowed me to feel it innocuously stowed away. Clad like movie stars walking the red carpet, we moved toward the entrance, the sound of our steps like the clop of hooves on rigid pavement. Wood steps that creaked like an old homestead in the dead of night led to a door lacking any grease for the hinges, paint peeled from exterior but not interior, lottery machines were occupied by three women and two men. Guys and gals sat at the bar, shoulder to shoulder and talking up a storm. To my right I could see a walkway leading to the noise of people calling their next shot as they played a game of 8-ball.

"Younger crowd, huh, Luis?"

"You do have to remember we are not as young as we once were." That was accurate, last time I went out I was a hell of a lot younger and did not have three granddaughters.

The barkeep came up, an Asian lady with tired eyes, olive-colored skin and black hair that was nappy, a tight shirt with nipples as hard as glass, she was older, younger than me, but not my type. "You want a drink?" she asked, trying to smile, but losing it far before she finished her short sentence.

"Course, that's why we came here, isn't it?" I asked Luis.

"Yes it is, I will take a vodka and cranberry, aka the Red Devil." Luis studied her face as she thought whether or not they had the ingredients.

"No cranberry, sorry."

"Do you have orange juice?"

"Ran out a half hour ago."

"Take a whiskey sour then," Luis tried to smile as well, though he too lost it long before his sentence was through.

"Do not have sour, she said."

Cutting in, I asked her, "You trying to prevent from serving us anything?"

She looked at me, offended, I could see black shadows under her eyes, long days spent and nights behind the bar making drinks for customers she did not like, longer nights counting money she did not own and had to pay back to the bank. I could tell she owned the joint. "Mistar, we do not 'ave." Her English was alright, I was able to understand at least.

"Take an old-fashioned," my turn to see what drinks she could make.

"Can't, not 'ave all ingredients."

"Seriously, what the hell do you have? Here, I will take that beer back there on tap." I directed her eyes with my finger drawn, pointing. A brown handle with white lettering rubbed off from ages where moist hands damp from the rag used to wipe the counter with, latched onto the tap handle and yanked it down to pour drinks.

"No keg, tap don't wook."

"I feel like I am fighting for a drink, what sort of place is this–you have just a whiskey?" Blood was leaving my face, white as a sheet and thirsty as a man walking the Sahara, I fought to quench my thirst.

"Yes." This time she did not bother to smile, her customers around the bar on stools glanced over at us as if we should've been anticipating this.

"Grab the bottle and put it on my tab." Our barkeep was about to run out of whiskey a hell of a lot sooner than predicted.

"Da ol ting?" she said as if it were not allowed.

"Yes, was I not clear?" Almost losing my temper, she came back with a cheaper bottle of Tennessee whiskey. Luis tried to stop me, he had an inkling of what I might do.

"I want 'top-shelf', not what you have there in your hands." Our bartender walked over and slid a step stool over, climbed and grabbed me the smooth whiskey I pointed at that came from Dublin. "Thank you, you sell cigarettes here?"

"'round the cornuh, sir, machean dispenses."

"Thank you." Luis grabbed me by the shoulder and walked me to the machine, frightened that I might send myself back to prison. Patrons were looking at Luis and I funny, like I had something on my face. Must be the suits, that's it. Inserting a quarter, I pressed the number that correlated to my pack of smokes and grabbed them below, bending my back and forcing a hand past the flap.

"This place is a piece of work, used to come here with the boys from work on occasion."

"Not how I remembered it either."

"See the floor over there," we moved into the pool hall area where five tables with green felt stood pretty, "worn to the hard wood beneath and sticky all around." (Carpet in a bar is tacky.)

"Critic, settle down we got you a bottle of whiskey," Luis said.

"Let's play a game, you said you have been working on your game since they locked me away." Smirking was all I could do, muscle memory does not fade that well when you hound a regimen into your brain for decades.

"That I have, let me grab some change, you select the cues." He walked back to the bar to exchange a dollar bill for change.

"These sticks are bowed like a bowlegged lanky sun-bitch," I said to no one in particular as I put stick after stick to the test, spinning them on the table to see if they were true, all of them wobbled. The tips were smashed good, I would just have to make do. The couple near Luis and I's table on the end were wearing sunglasses in the joint, behind tinted lenses I could not see their gaze, but I knew they took a gander at me like many before. I packed my cigarettes by tapping the twenty of them hard against the palm of my hand, opened and grabbed a fresh candidate to place in the side of my mouth, Luis came back just in time.

"Can I use your lighter, pal?" He tossed me a book of matches to get me by. "Thanks, the cues are dreadful."

"Why's that?"

"Bowed like that stripper who slapped titties in my face."

"Oh, damn. Must be bad then." I handed him one, he took it to the table and tested it the same as I, "This the best they have?"

"Far as I could see, if there were a better one, someone else is using it at the moment."

"Here, you rack the balls." He put change in the stiff mechanism and crunched it in, jerked it out, the balls dropped and rolled down the slope to where I could get at them.

"Slow, takes about as long for me to take a piss at my old age as it does for this table to get the balls out."

"I know what you mean, fucking prostate. If there were one true punishment to man it would be that, doc says keep your point down, don't drink so much, eat healthier. The older you get, the more of a bitch everything turns out to be." Luis poured us both a glass of whiskey, the glasses were cheap plastic with wavy marks from the heat cooking them as if dried outside.

"Tastes better outside bars," I said as I took a long dramatic sip.

"Everything is better outside of prison, Hank."

"Not everything."

"What do you mean?"

"Poetry."

"How so?"

"Pain, suffering, it's all there, in whomever walks by. The fuel for the richest poetry is derived from agony. The best I have written is made solely from affliction."

Luis took a slug from his glass and covered his mouth as he belched. "Oh, I see." He tilted his gaze down at his glass and then finished it off. "You want another?"

"Fill it up, old friend." He did, I racked the balls on the table, flipped a coin to see who broke, Luis called heads and it was tails, so I broke.

Like a slingshot, the cue ball propelled down the table and spread out the triangle, it had been a long time, but it appears I had not lost my touch, as Luis exclaimed, "8-ball on break?"

"Practice can only do so much good, talent baby." That was a quick game, "Rack 'em up." He did, I broke again, this time sinking three stripes, I called the next shot and the next one, made the rest of my balls in and sunk the 8 in the side pocket.

"Are you even going to let me have a shot?"

"Depends."

"On?"

"Rack it up again, you have to catch up two games now." He racked and I broke, took it easier this time and only made four on the first go.

"Solids?"

"Yeah, don't hit the stripes in, I hate charity." I sipped on my drink and watched him play, we were halfway through the fifth of whiskey with a quarter-filled glass apiece. Luis shot the 2 ball down the table into a corner pocket, cue ball set behind the 8 and wedged between the wall, his 3 was dormant at the other end near the corner pocket.

"3, corner," he called, focusing on his shot. He banked it off the bumper and the cue ball strode down the table magnificently to tap in his 3. I smacked the table with a hand and dropped ash on the floor, not giving a lick, Damon, that son of bitch taught me a few habits I still have today.

Blowing smoke out of my nostrils, I said, "Practice makes perfect, that was perfect. You have been warming up."

"For too damn long." Luis tied the game, took the lead and beat me. We played games until our whiskey ran out, the last match we called for the night had us set at a dead even tie, Luis had the cue ball sitting on the edge of a corner pocket, about to fall in and not a straight shot or even a feasible shot to make at the 8.

"Masse?"

"Yeah, Hank, Masse shot it is." The Masse shot is where you apply extreme English by elevating the cue stick anywhere from a 30 to a 90-degree angle. Skilled players can do it, I can, Luis could barely hold the stick last I played with him. Lining up, the 8 sat on the side pocket three inches out, Luis struck the cue ball and it spun a maddening spin—chaotic, grazing the 8 just enough, the ball moved as if time were slowed down, and it went in.

Game.

"Lost, Hank, looks like practicing did me right." If that was not the most smartass response to winning, I don't know truthfully what would be. I felt a placid assurance from Luis, he had changed.

Dignified as I could for how furious I was, "Good game, buddy." We shook hands and both left out to my car, I never paid for the bottle of whiskey and I hadn't planned on it, never would I subject myself to a low standard bar again.

Liquor store closed, I cursed and asked Luis, "You have any more liquor in here?" It was getting close to 1:00 a.m., I still planned on celebrating. Hell, wait twenty-five years for a day and you should intend for an all-nighter.

"No, but there is a house party a couple blocks down from my place." I swerved in the road and kept my eyes peeled.

"Are you going to arrest me, officer, for swerving?"

"No, I am a Carlton cop, Hank, we just harass people and give speeding tickets–besides, I am off the clock."

"This house party, people our age going to be there?"

"Mostly, hard to say, it is at Cleveland's."

"Seriously? That dumb motherfucker."

"Hank, they have booze for free."

"Seems how you blew a month's pay on suits and accessories. I presume we are in need of free drinks."

"Sharp as ever, it won't be that bad."

"He still look the same?"

"The pictures I showed you were out of date, just wait."

"As if it were to be some sort of surprise seeing his piteous ass."

Carlton, it had changed in moderation. Businesses down the main strip were new and freshly painted, wineries moved in and took over more area, the fire department was transformed into a wine seller and murals were decorating the sides of buildings on the corners. The tracks I laid down were still there and operational, Carlton's train station was clean and tidy as last I saw. We went straight to Luis's house to drop off my car and walk down to Cleveland's dwelling. Luis's deputy was asinine, he likely would try to handcuff me for driving in a straight line, better not to risk parking my pride and joy in the vicinity of where we would be drinking and near Cleveland.

On the way. I saw morning dew sparkle, stumbling, I started to smoke a cigarette, "Cleveland better not be a jackass. He ain't worth putting up with to take his drink."

"He is not that bad, Hank, relax, smoke your smoke and relax." I have had friends in prison mention that someone was "not that bad" and when you see their record for what they are in for, it curdles your innards and it has you wishing they were sentenced to death row.

"There better not be an orgy going on and we run into it in the midst, or some freaky sadist bonding party."

"You have an imagination, no, if there is, I am going to start shooting dicks if it gets in the way while we go for a bottle to take."

"That is what I like to hear, tenacity. Take his drinks and leave."

"If there is food, I might eat some first."

"My stomach is rumbling, nerves have had me in a racket."

"Just enjoy your cigarette and take it easy, Hank, no need to stress yourself out about nothing." I nodded and we kept moving forward.

Five minutes later, a drunk came out of the dark with a tie around his neck, "You see Misty, you there?" he asked Luis with a bottle of whiskey in his hand, bumbling.

"Misty? Who might that be and who are you?"

"I am Ernest. Have you seen her, my girlfriend?"

"No. Hank, you?"

I turned my head clockwise in a three-sixty and saw not hide nor hair, "Nothing, can I have a drink?"

"She left me," Ernest said, "I cheated on her, I shouldn't 'ave." Cheats, I hate them, despicable.

"Can I have a pull off your bottle, Ernest?"

"Here, have some," he handed it to me, I smiled, "you guy's going somewhere?"

"Party down the street," Luis said.

"Mind if I tag along?"

"If you share your drink, sure," I told him, the kind of friend who only is around for pleasure and nothing else.

34

Earnest was thirty-two, four years ago he was released from the military with a purple heart. A victim of a bombing accident, he had a cracked skull patched by a shoddy plate, screws can be felt if you don't mind the scar, he says. Misty, his girlfriend, or was, Earnest was uncertain of either at the moment, partially afraid his woman up and left him for another man without PTSD and who would not commit infidelity in a relationship. Claiming that sleeping with her sister was not his fault at all, inebriated as he was at the time, the sister of Misty came in the occupied bathroom downstairs, stripped and began to shower along with him; catching Earnest by surprise he had understood that now since she was already in the shower that he would be manipulated if not partaking in intercourse, so he said, either way he was screwed literally and figuratively. And when caught in the act, the sister ran as Misty commenced wailing on Earnest with his belt that had been haphazardly laying across the toilet tank. By the time Earnest had withdrawn the belt from her grasp, he had already received a few gashes to his cheek from the buckle and numerous marks around his torso. While trying to discuss what had happened, Earnest was dressing himself, by the time he had the tie on she yanked on it till his eyes felt like they might pop, he fainted, woke up and she was gone. Taking a fifth of whiskey from his liquor cabinet, he started to drink until she came back, she had not for two nights, so he went out searching. That is when Luis and I ran into him.

Cleveland had a robust build since last I saw him, a receding hairline that left a small tuft in the center where his widow's peak was. He too wore a suit, not as nice as Luis's or mine, but close. His wife Meredith was model quality to my surprise, for an older lady about forty-five, she was every bit a diamond in the rough here. I thought about sweet-talking her into removing her dress, smart enough to know myself, I decided not to bother, adultery is a forte I refrain from.

A new housing development was set near a barren field overlooking a vineyard in the far distance. Carlton had changed, I skipped driving over the bridge earlier to see whether Luis was pulling my leg about what happened to the lake. I had been standing at the front door with Luis and Earnest ready to crash Cleveland's party if he would let us in. His wife gave me a wide-eyed look, I knew she was interested, but this old puppy was not on the market. My heart just hasn't been right since Maybelline, I can view a specimen, though as far as engaging with one, I am hard-pressed not to stir up memories, memories that haunt me into the night.

"Cleveland, good to see you. I decided to come by for your party and friends tagged along, may we come in?" Luis said with a drunken smile. We had finished the bottle Earnest had on him and tossed it out in the neighbor's rhododendron bush.

"Hey," he said, ecstatic, "you came!" Cleveland hugged Luis, squeezing the air out of him, popping his back loudly to my ears' discontent. "Chief, I mean. Salute," he saluted and Luis smacked himself in the face. "Welcome, you have friends, I see."

"Don't we all, in high places and in low," I told him sarcastically.

"And who might you be? You're familiar..." A look an officer gives bore down on me, speculative, judging, and curious.

"Hank, Hank Shine. How do you do?" My voice denied any disgust I truthfully felt for Cleveland, some individuals have an aura about them you can't stand, the fact he could be a veritable dick was another facet to the scale tipping towards the "I don't goddamn like you one bit" side.

For the booze, I would hide my dissatisfaction.

"That's it," the figurative light bulb flicked on in his mind, "you were driving drunk on my first day." What really irritated me was that

Cleveland chose this time to start pointing at me as if I were a child molester at the park, searching for my next victim. "I was going to give you a ticket, but Luis told me not to," his eyes diverted over to Luis with stark gander.

"For a damn good reason too," Luis said. As a small town chief, he had the power of the law and seldom would he carry out disreputable actions, the times that he had was for me. Earnest had our flank, hooking his thumbs in the front pocket of his black leather jacket.

"Yeah, otherwise I would've shoved your ten-gallon hat up your pretentious ass." Luis smirked at that, but tried not to have it noticed, I only smiled a smile I did not feel.

"Tried, you would have tried, logically it would not work so," Cleveland was sure proud of his wit.

The gruesome details were revealed, "Where there is a will there's a way. Anyhow, let us just leave the past in the past." A slight murmur escaped the deputy's lips.

"What'd you say, Cleveland?"

"Luis, this man was the reason you were not supposed to show up tonight. You let a convict come to my home?"

"Ex-convict, Cleveland, if you do not want to be plumbing porcelain thrones and detailing the cruisers from sun up to sun down, you best leave it at that," every ounce of authority in his voice.

"Yes, yes sir. You must be famished here, come in." I was thirsty, I knew that.

"Earnest," I said, "don't trust that guy."

"Why is that, Hank?" He was not the intellectual I was desiring him to be, a simple man, sometimes that is alright. Wisdom comes to those that wait and observe rather than force the notion.

"Just best not to," I put a cigarette in my mouth and lit it, mumbling, "okay."

Cars were parked out front, for a double-wide trailer the capacity was at its maximum. Friends of Cleveland were drinking shots in the living room at a multi-colored coffee table, five trays of jello shots were spread out on the dining table with half of them eaten, bottles of whiskey, brandy, tequila, vodka, and gin were either empty or full and scattered throughout the kitchen. Before asking, I grabbed a cold beer from an ice tub near the fridge and popped the top while Luis entertained Cleveland by the entrance. Cleveland's wife came into the kitchen where Ernest and I stood chasing liquor with beer.

"You are handsome, a woman ever told you that before, Mr. Shine?" She fluttered her long eyelashes at me like I was her crush.

"To be honest, not as many as you would think." And that had been the truth, not too many have said it, being a married man and in a relationship prior to marriage for several years, I was not inclined to interact with women due to respect for my wife. Women have come and gone, leaving compliments that lead nowhere.

"Consider me one of the rare ones," she said, flirtatious for a woman married to a cop, bad news any way you perceive it.

"I could, what makes you rare?" I eyed her over my beer bottle as I gulped some down.

"Rare, hmm…" she sucked on her bottom lip and removed lipstick in the process, "I suppose individuality. See, I am not quite like anyone else."

"Good answer, rare answer, it suits you … Meredith."

"You know my name?" Saying that as if it were absurd.

"Luis told me Cleveland's wife was named Meredith and I only put two and two together while I saw you at the door greeting new guests. Thank you for your hospitality, madam," I said, dignified as if this were not some manufactured double-wide with cardboard trim and an asshole named Cleveland living here.

"Much obliged, Hank, would you care to get shown around the house?" If that was not a cry for a quick session in the master bedroom, I frankly am unsure what was. She wanted it, hell, I had been in prison restrained from any intercourse for nearly half my existence. The proposition did intrigue me, but it fell short of pursuit at the moles on her neck and predator eyes I felt ready to eat me alive. Next thing I need is to have my best friend catch me with my pants down in his deputy's house, though I would like to put it to Cleveland like that, I prefer to stay out of sticky situations that are likely to get me shot.

I gave her a blank expression, "No, not really, would you care to take a few shots with me instead?"

"Have you had a jello shot?" A cook at heart was always proud of their work, whether it be cupcakes or jello shots, "I made them myself, easier than one would think and it hits the spot," she winked as if it were a que for me to follow her around like a dog on a leash, that or she had been attacked by an invisible bug.

"No, not a jello kinda guy." Prison serves jello as a dessert three nights a week, that and tapioca. Scarred for life, I passed on the opportunity to relive memories I had yet the time to suppress sufficiently. "I am sure they are good."

"Good? They are fantastic. You must try one," I view desperation from a perspective where pestiferous acts are the key element, Meredith was desperate for me. Neglected by her dullard husband was the precursor to why I assume she was longing for something I just couldn't give, not anymore.

"Sorry, I just am not in the mood. Whiskey or gin?" Two bottles of varying sizes in my hand, the gin was a half-gallon of bottom-shelf spit. However, the whiskey was to my liking when I took a whiff.

"Both," hardcore alcoholics as I am can take shots of assorted spirits in the same sitting.

"Earnest, what do you want?"

Slouched over the counter and with sheer will holding his eyelids apart, "Both sound fine."

"Both it is, grab us some shot glasses and I'll pour." Each grabbed two shot glasses, I filled them to the rim. With Meredith's assistance, I found clean shot glasses near the sink.

"Alright, one, two," she smacked her hand down on the counter top, "three." The three of us tossed back a shot, then the next.

"Another?" I asked.

Earnest, of course, drinking out of misery, "Yes."

"You boys can drink."

"I am afraid I am not a boy anymore, sweetheart," my tired old face met her younger and harmless expression.

DIARY OF A DEAD MAN

"Appears not, pour another." I did, delighted too. Here I was thinking I was going to have to run in here, steal a bottle and leave. To my delight, I had not been kicked out yet, that is a good sign in my book. Being barred from a bar is humiliating, the door to a home hitting your ass on the way out is devastating.

"One, two, three," she counted off; on three we took a shot of whiskey, then one of gin, cringing at the mixture, I relented.

"Alright," changing my mind, "let us try a jello shot, something to wash the taste of gin out of my mouth."

"You do not like gin?" Meredith asked, confused.

"Sporadically I do, tonight was sporadic. Not my cup of tea, tastes better mixed in tonic water, in my opinion."

"Are you opinionated, Mr. Shine?"

"Just call me, Hank, doll. A man with a mind and heart has an opinion, fairly I would say so. Earnest, are you opinionated?"

"Depends on what we might be talking about," he was drunk and wobbling like a top about to fall.

"Understandable," I feasted my eyes on red, blue, and orange jello shots in small paper condiment dishes, "let's see what you have to say about the jello."

"What color would you care to try, Hank?" Meredith looked at me with lust.

"Orange, yeah, how about that first." I looked over my shoulder to see Luis keeping his deputy busy discussing work and whatever else he could. Luis knew I did not tolerate Cleveland too well, if I was sober, I'd bury him alive.

"Is orange your favorite color?" She asked.

"No, green actually," I said.

"Mine is purple." I did not really care, but I acted as if I did.

"Very well, thanks." She handed me an orange one, I licked the edge to break free the jello and was content with masking the taste of gin. "Not bad at all, young lady, did you use vodka?"

Meredith just finished eating a blue one, "Yes, sir. Another?"

"One more, have to see how fast they creep up."

"Orange?"

"No, take a blue this time." She handed me one more and I nodded, Earnest was sucking them down, free was free. Licking my lips, I was surprised that they tasted great.

"How was it?" Meredith smiled expectantly, knowing my bias for jello to be soon quieted and thought of in a new light.

"Wonderful, you are a woman of many talents. Jello can taste rather straightforward, bland, and artificial. In my book, you worked a miracle here, changing this old dog's view. I would have to say if I ever were to be fixing for a batch of jello, I'd come here and bother you." Lying like a snake, I created a fake story, "I had the ones at the bar in the past when there was a special going on, yours are absolutely stunning in comparison."

"Why, thank you, I spent all of last night preparing them, so to see the endpoint of this night in a positive way is truly heartening." She put her hand on my hand, "If you will excuse me, I need to use the ladies room." She walked away, good, time for me to grab a bottle or two and walk out the door. I was tired of her hounding me for a quick fuck, what did I look desperate? My appearance is not so, it must be the suit, a woman loves a fine-dressed man as I have been told and noticed a time or two.

"Earnest, pick your poison, let's go outside and have a smoke." He stood before the alcohol bottles and pinched his chin while in thought, decision made, he grabbed a fifth of vodka that was near capacity. I reached for a bottle of whiskey, shoved a glass in my pocket and took a fifth of brandy under one arm. You may as well walk out with style if you are going to walk out at all. "Alright, let's go have us a smoke outside while Luis continues to keep Cleveland entertained talking about arresting three lazy hookers a month, if that, in this Podunk town."

"Roger that, got stogies in my jacket," Earnest patted his pocket.

"Ah, those? Thanks, but no thanks, you can smoke those all you want. I prefer a filtered cigarette myself, pal." Cigars were great when I was in the mood, my mentality as of now had me focused on my habitual patterns: drinking whiskey and smoking filtered cigarettes. A comforting combination that adhered to me like super glue.

"Suit yourself," Earnest said. The guests were preoccupied playing a game of 21 on the coffee table over a bottle of Hennessy I gagged at the sight of. Marique had insisted we drink Hennessy twice a week, I didn't even want to drink it once for that matter. Luis nodded at me seeing the bottles and grabbed Cleveland by the shoulder to take him over to the card game.

"How does this game work, Cleveland?" Luis said, like a fool.

"You mean you have never played? Let me get you involved next hand, here is a five, chief, to get you started." A sweaty bill was placed in Luis's palm, face up.

"Going to have a smoke, catch you outside in a little, too stuffy in here for this old man," I said as I hurried out the door, brandy under one arm and whiskey held to the side avoiding contact with Cleveland. He seemed more determined to avoid any such confrontation with me, I was a cockroach he could not crush under the weight of his boot, he was elated that I saved him the trouble and walked out on my own. I did not plan on coming back in, I would sit outside until Luis finished cleaning up the water he muddied for a diversion. Luis did not mind playing cards with me, he said to me once, but most take the game too seriously and he just preferred to play at leisure.

35

There was a derelict moss-covered bench to the side of the house where we could not be seen, I took a load off while Earnest twitched around drinking straight from the bottle. He pulled out a stogie and started it with a match I removed from the box Luis had gifted to me earlier. Likewise, I lit up my cigarette and challenged decrepit lungs to endure the haze drifting in and out. When there were fewer days that I had smoked–when I started, my lungs were bottomless. Now, I could use an oxygen tank.

Earnest slurped his vodka down like a Russian, when he spoke I could have sworn I heard an accent. I took a drink from the glass I nicked and studied the stars ahead, this went on for about ten minutes while Earnest talked about Misty, girl problems were not my forte. Hard to believe, but I am worse than most men when it comes to handling problems with their significant others, see I don't know how to compromise, there is no going back after certain events transpire. If I could have Earnest understand one thing, it would be that after he cheated, he should move on. His relationship would only get toxic, make him sick to the bone, and deprive him of ambition.

Barely holding himself up, Earnest started to push my buttons, "You know, when I was in the war we had to do things," he told me as if I were giving out stars, here, you get a gold one for sharing actual war stories. At a time like this–the first one in twenty-five years outside of the cage–I did

175

not care in the slightest to discuss matters of war, brutality, treachery, not even about his girlfriend. In truth, I wanted to sit back and relax, enjoy the greener grass, smoke and drink to my heart's content.

"You don't say." Uninterested, I switched my gaze from that of Earnest back to a more enticing sky. There was a haze floating like clouds, more than likely pollution at its finest. The North Star seared one's vision, from where I was positioned, I could see it at the top of a tree like an ornament.

"Some men," he swayed like a boat at sea, "figured killing them over-seas was horrible, I think it was necessary." Necessary, killing another human, I had been there in prison where it was either my ass or theirs, I had chosen theirs.

It did not matter this time what I said, so I repeated myself to show my enthusiasm caustically, "You don't say." His hands thrown up in the air, vodka sterilizing his skin and washing away the jello from his front teeth where it was fixed a second ago.

"Horrible is on how you conceptualize absurdity." Earnest was losing my attention fast, speaking of killing people was a topic I cared the least to speak of, considering I had experienced it first hand. There is nothing to speak about, you kill someone, that is it, it is on your hands, you die with that knowledge. Stirring up memories was a quick attack to dimin-ishing the good vibes I had created today walking through the gates and driving my coupe with Luis riding along.

"Keep it for yourself, pal."

"You know, I killed a lot of men with these two hands," he raised them, looking at them as I did now too with them shoved in my face. Scars and stitch marks, burn marks, hash-marked knuckles and nails that had residue underneath. "Some may have been innocent, we did it for our country. Our country, you see, to keep the people safe, to save fellow men, we killed who we had to at the time. I killed many men," he ram-bled on like the guy at the bar interrupting the game on the radio, "more than most, I had a count of eighty-two. Snipers in the forces had higher counts than I, considering how long I was in there, I was labeled as an efficient killer. Our government trained me, paid me, housed me, fed me, they took care of me as long as I was of use to them … until the accident.

Until I was unfit for tactical measures, when the bomb went off, everything changed. I was too weak for war, too weak for them. My country, I would do anything for it, I would be there you see, killing the enemies to this day. Whether it be man, woman or child. I did what had to be done, for our sovereignty. There is no credit for a man like me out here, I am looked at with sad eyes, the mark of who I am is seen. Kill them all, kill all of them, go wild into the abyss and never come back, for my country I would do it again and again until there was truly no 'get up and go' left in these weary bones."

"Really, stop." He was making me sick, but he did not realize, talking to himself practically. There is a point in a conversation, particularly when you are drunk and smoking, that it is an excess, be concise and save it. Make it too wordy and you lose your audience, have it be controversial, that too will lose your audience. Since I was the only one in the audience, he lost me when he first started smacking his lips.

"I had to, I wanted to. For my country, little boys came at times," my blood tasted of copper as I bit my cheeks, coated my tongue and held contempt in my demeanor as Earnest spoke ludicrously, "I killed them with bullets, tore holes through them for my country–"

"Knock it the fuck off, Earnest," I said extremely disinterested. "Speak of slaughtering for our country somewhere else. This is not the time or the place, you want to go share your old war stories, fine, share them where I am not around. Lock yourself in a closet and let it out, do it where nobody has to listen, that would be best, just do it somewhere else."

"What, are you not a patriot?" Tears started to fall from his face, he was losing it, he laughed, that maniacal laugh that projects when you reach your limit as a human being. I was creeped out and partially tempted to chuck my bottle of brandy at his forehead and put him to rest, drag him to the ditch and leave him there.

"What I am and what I am not is none of your damn business. Speaking about the dead is not appropriate at the level in which you are speaking. You bury that down in, you never surface it.

"Leave, you are not welcome here."

"For my country, to defend against those who disapprove," in the blink of an eye like a trained killer, he engaged the hammer on a six-shooter with a wood grip, I could see the insanity in his eyes, "a true patriot does not stand by idly while one of our fellow men disapproves of what is necessary in time of war." The barrel found its way to my temple, leaving an indent and, who knows, a hole.

"War, keep that shit for yourself, you psychotic nut." I glared at him with strong animosity, took a sip of my drink and set the glass down next to me, pulled a cigarette out and started to smoke, "You would be doing me a favor."

"Huh?" He said shaky. Adrenaline will do that to you, he was on a rush right now, transferable through the air. I held my peace and kept as tranquil as possible under the implications.

"Saving me the trouble of doing it later," I said, harsh and unflinching. "Pull the trigger, pussy, pull it, fucking pull it, take fate into your own hands. Shoot. You have the power of God in your hands, the Almighty, don't be a fool and pull out your toy if you are not going to follow through. You're a warrior, aren't you, been through hell for our country, kill another man if you see it fit, kill me or step the fuck away and leave."

"You want me to?" He wanted to, thought I was testing him, I could tell.

"Sure, why the heck not? Put one through my brain–let's play Russian Roulette, I am not afraid are you." The barrel had been cold at first, my skin warmed the metal and now it and I were at equal temperatures.

"No," he said, and looked like a child tested to their full ability.

"What are you waiting for, do it, pussy." His hand started to stagger, scraping my flesh, "For your country." Instigating a man such as Earnest was not the smartest thing I had done, but not the dumbest either, sadly.

"Uhhhh…" This was do or die, pull the trigger and execute or walk away. His eyes darted back and forth, his pores were open and I could smell the sweat. Earnest pissed himself too, the viscera got to him, he was no more prepared for this than a common citizen, I was ready to die whenever Mother Nature wanted to reclaim my body.

"If you are not going to do it, hand me the gun and allow myself the pleasure, that or walk the fuck away!" I was tired of assholes wasting my time, last thing I wanted was to be arrested for killing Earnest for threatening my life, that would go over really well in court. First night out, I bash a young man's skull in with my fists until I cause boxer fractures and split skin, I'd beat him to a bloody pulp the same as Josiah had for a vendetta over forty years ago. It would not be hard to kill Earnest while he contemplated. With refined skill at hand-to-hand combat, I could snap his neck if my joints allowed me to move limber for an instant.

He busted down crying, "I … I'm so … rry."

"Save it for someone who gives a damn," he put the gun down, "leave before I take your gun and frame you for shooting me in the brain. Go on, scat!" At this time, I yelled and he ran, I resumed stargazing and sat there until Luis came out ten minutes later.

"You alright, Hank?" Luis asked.

"Peachy. I ran out of smokes, can I bum one?"

"Here."

"Thanks," I started chain-smoking.

"You look miffed?"

"Ah, it's nothing, posers trying to grow a set."

"What happened to—"

"Earnest, he ran home."

"Why?" I passed him a fifth of brandy to take a slug from as we spoke.

"Fear of using other peoples' bathrooms, apparently."

With speculation, he asked, "Why did he not just go outside?"

"Number two, he said he was not a dog. I asked him the same thing, oh well." Pushing the ordeal aside, I said, "Let's get back to my car and go drink at my place." He let it slide and started heading back, telling me how he won seventy bucks playing 21 and did not reimburse Cleveland. His deputy was more interested earning brownie points with his superior than he was losing money. I told him how Meredith seemed quite fond of me, how she wanted to give me a tour of the spread. Luis only latched around my neck and started to smash my hair down with a fist and stopped to chortle.

36

onths went by, my home was not a home anymore. Wife gone, kids gone, their stuff all gone. I took Maybelline's belongings and left them in a garbage sack outside the local Baptist church. Holding onto her items was only holding onto old memories, I could do without most of them, the bad that is. There was good in our relationship for quite some time, the happiest I was in my life was with her before she cheated on me. The dagger to my heart set us down an unsteady road with only the future for the kids in sight, inconsequential was our marriage if not for the fact of the three boys.

There were things to be grateful for, namely, Luis had taken outstanding care of the place while I was sitting in a cell. To my excitement, he regularly dusted and vacuumed like any good housemaid. Leaves were raked and trees were trimmed, hedges had been whacked clean to a stump, minor landscaping had been implemented. I noticed my library had been organized and the 45 rpm records I kept in ancient beer cases had been organized to boot. A fresh set of clothes had been washed, folded, and placed on my bedside where the sheets smelled of new detergent. Picking up the clothes at the time, there was a brand new flask strapped to a bottle of whiskey with a rubber band, I removed the rubber band and started to drink immediately.

There was a special surprise waiting for me in the backyard. Luis dropped it off while I was nursing my hangover in bed the next day after attending Cleveland's shindig, a dog. She was an American Staffordshire Terrier puppy, three months of age. I was pleased to see that the bitch's ears weren't docked for fighting. Her tail was left at inherent length, she was an energetic little shit that sure grew up fast and filled the void in my heart as much as feasible. I named her Cleo, she listened well and could give a rendition of tricks from playing dead to walking on her hind legs for a treat.

Cleo came to be my best friend next to Luis. We were inseparable, she trotted on four paws the size of my closed fist, Cleo had my back and growled at folk who threatened her comfort or mine. Cleo would lay on my back while I was sprawled on the couch or recliner, all I would do was whistle at her if she were sniffing about, say "get my back girl, come on, get my back", and sure enough Cleo ran and wedged herself.

A week after I was released, Luis gave me the specs on where James would take his daughters to play, it was close to home too. I lurked behind an alder in Carlton by the lower park's river. A hundred feet from the play structure I could see my oldest son for the first time in a long time, James was a full-grown man. His face was masked with a lined and defined beard, edged with a straight razor, as I presume, and trimmed in a delicate procedure. James's shoulders were broad as a barn, muscle left impressions under his tight white T-shirt, hair hung down below the jaw. He dressed casually with black pants and matching belt with a silver buckle.

My son sat down on a blanket and opened a picnic basket to remove a bottle of wine and a crystal glass, some cheese and a roll of crackers. He sat there peacefully, wise, and observant of his daughters. Three precious girls around the age of ten played on the swings, two were the same age and one the youngest. While swinging, they conversed about an elementary writing class where the teacher did not show up, he was sick, is what they said. Mr. Kan was his name, he was always sick as they clarified, very friendly as well.

Hiding beneath my rib cage, my heart broke as I saw the three darling girls, all with curly dark hair, head over to the slide, climb the steps as James had before, and slide down with a belly full of laughter. Naive and congruent, I hoped they would not have to face the harsh realities of life. I took James here before, he must really like the place, some memories do not expunge. Curiosity killed the cat, I am curious why he chose this park specifically as a routine, a question I will take to my grave.

The mother to my grandchildren came out of an outhouse near the gravel parking lot and walked over. She was all of five feet, had tan arms, smooth legs that showed due to her short skirt and sleeveless shirt. Strawberry blonde hair was braided into pigtails, lain across one shoulder, the other awkwardly locked between b-cups. Her stride was relaxed, confident, she had purpose in moving forward to return to her jovial family.

Ashamed of my cowardice, I decided that they would be better off without me, after all that I had done. They were happy, I had a prudent feeling James did not want me in their life, if he had, he would've responded to a letter. In twenty-five years, each one of my sons received a letter every week. Not a single one came to visit, Luis was the only person who came to see me and for that, to at least have him, I was thankful.

My son Johnny, a slender man that bore his mother's grace, worked a used car lot. I walked up and could smell the alcohol on his breath; as we spoke over a domestic coupe I acted like I was interested in buying. We stood there and smoked a few cigarettes, he chatted about politics, how the President was a shithead, his wife a tramp, and his sons mollycoddled twats. I held tears back, not blowing my cover, how sad to stand before your own flesh and blood and for them to have no clue who you are. For his time, I slipped him a crisp Benjamin Franklin, we drank a few beers around the corner at a bar way past its expiration date. Johnny knew me as Brice Coalfield, a friendly gentleman with a drinking problem. My son had a girl on the side wrapped around his finger as he told me, and had been seeing her for quite some time. Taking out his wallet, he removed a photo of her, Nia, her name was Nia, she was something else. Black hair and brown eyes, wavy and feathered back behind sweet little ears that fit her face. My eyes started to water at the sight of her, I told him she was beautiful and that I was happy for him.

Kid had a hard life, I could tell, much the same as I had, a curse I passed along to those who were supposed to be closest to me. Johnny was a good salesman, just not good enough, not today, we walked back to the car lot. I stashed the business card he handed me, thanked him for drinking with me and bit my tongue. He too would be better off without me.

Walt was working the counter at an automotive parts store in McMinnville. With copper irises, he looked just like his father and had a part of Maybelline in the mix too. I walked up to Walt and asked for windshield wipers for the coupe and a carburetor kit, he was good at his job. I tipped him a twenty and walked out the door, just could not bear unsettling him either.

May would have liked to see how they all turned out, turned out better than we ever were. All were at peace in their routines. Who was I to bother, to shift the sand, to change the way they had lived their lives since I had been gone and they moved on. I killed their mother and left them to fend for themselves. I wanted to be the best father and husband, dreamed to be, sometimes dreams do not come true. In a way, I felt gutless, I also felt that I was doing the right thing for once, not disturbing anyone. How the times have changed, I, a grandfather and May, she would've been a magnanimous grandmother if alive to this date.

Damn.

37

B y the time I was seventy-three, not much new had occurred, I
tried to keep peace and an easy life, kept my neck out of other
peoples' problems and focused on my writing. My poetry was
published under a pseudonym, along with a few novels about fiction-
al characters portraying Oregon, the setting for three of them were in
Portland and one in McMinnville. The final book I am working on right
now portrays my life in the form of a diary of a sort.

Cleo was my company more than anyone else, during the night Luis
would come over and visit, drink with me and reminisce. He retired
at sixty-five and has spent the years hence constructing boats as a hobby, while I sit there pulling his leg and leisurely reading a good book. I
stopped by and spoke with Walt about auto parts every so often, bothered Johnny over a car I would never buy, and kept tabs on my eldest son.
His daughters graduated beauty college and now owned a beauty salon
down Third Street where Damon and I used to go to the strip club at.

For about six months, I had been coughing up blood, it started with
a small amount and in time grew to be too much, I could not bear to
be stubborn and avoid the doc any longer. The opium I was smoking at
night did not take away the suffering, it was time for me to go visit Dr.
Judd. He decided to wait to tell me what the prognosis was until the results were sent back, in the meantime, I started injecting morphine to put

myself at ease, like any good junkie. Deplorably, the first time I used it, I blacked out to awake several hours later retching on myself. Each time after, I became less queasy. Blood still spewed out of me like a beast from hell, incidentally, I stopped wearing white shirts and only wore black, that was fine, I liked dark material.

A month ago I went to see Dr. Judd for test results, you can tell something is not right when your doctor takes a long while to render the consequential news. Judd stood there before me in a white coat, navy blue stethoscope like a necklace around his neck and round glasses at the peak of his pug nose, holding a folder, hangdog, folding one sleeve up, then the opposite, perusing my results.

"You don't look so hot, Hank." I had a handkerchief in my hand, my face was white as a sheet of paper or a sheep's ass, I was going for the sheep's ass look. Coughing until the back of my throat stung, blood came up and dispersed onto the cloth in my hand.

"Eh, you know me. Always feeling splendid. You could use some makeup yourself, Doctor Judd." He laughed at me and tried to hold the same tone, sad at my emaciated body, dropping twenty pounds since my last visit; still kept a chipper attitude as not to get anyone down in the dumps; to cross a sick puppy is a sorrowful sight.

"I'd have to borrow some of yours," we chuckled.

"Threw it out with the rest of my wife's stuff, sorry."

"No hard feelings. Let's get down to business, Hank," Judd said, with a look of regret.

"Yeah, yeah, let's hear it, doc. What juicy details do you have to disclose?" I snapped my fingers and coughed some more.

"After the endoscopic exam of your esophagus, the results were not what I was hoping for," I thought he was going to cry, he really loved his job, but hated this part of it, there are always pros and cons in life. "You have cancer, as we suspected, however, more severe than we had anticipated: stage four. Malignant tumors are spreading rampantly throughout your body, Hank, in your lymph glands, your lungs, it's grievous, Hank. Your body is like a pinball machine and the pinball is cancer, it is running its course." The analogy started a wry smile on my face, Judd was a clever man. "So egregious, we…" he had trouble forming the words, so I spoke for him.

"It's okay, doc," I said, reassuringly.

"Hank, we can't do anything. You are going to die." I laughed, man did I laugh and spray blood around the joint in a sad, sad way. My whole life had been foreboding, this was nothing new.

"Judd, we are all destined to die sooner or later. Spare yourself the anguish, look at me," he did, "I will be fine."

"No, no you won't, Hank. You have a month left to live, if that. You will choke to death, on your own blood," he said seriously, as if it were the hardest thing he had ever had to tell a patient.

"A month?" I rubbed my hands together, making friction.

"Yes," his expression grave.

I smiled, "Hell, that is a lot more than some and a lot less than most. No despair, I will play my cards. Choking to death, you say?" He was not sure how to take it, he looked at me peculiarly.

"Yes, on your own blood, Hank. It will not be pretty."

"Most things in life aren't, and people have died in worse ways. My time was due a long way back." Philosophical in nature, I spread my wisdom, the short amount I had scavenged over the decades.

"Would you like to pray together, Mr. Shine?" His faith would not do any good for me now.

"God can't save me now and, if he were to, I would be damned pissed at him. This is my time to go, if any, the last pages on my manuscript are about to be finished. I might just have enough time."

"I'd like to read your book when you finish, Hank," he put a hand on mine.

"You will, just don't inform Luis what is going on if he calls. I know I have him listed under emergency contacts."

"Doctor patient confidentiality, you have no need to worry."

"Good, I knew I could trust you, doc. Now, what kind of drugs can I get to cope with this catastrophe?" I grinned like a kid in a candy store.

"I will refill your morphine prescription, and assign you methadone as well. Don't O.D. on me either, Hank."

"I won't, I have a book to finish. I just need something to get me by, you see."

"What is your book's title?" Judd had pen and paper in hand and was ready to jot down the information.

"Diary Of A Dead Man." We held each other's gaze.

"Oh, I see. How fitting."

"Certainly," I grabbed my slips for the narcotics. "Judd, I am afraid this will be the last time I see you."

"I know, I am sorry, Hank."

"Don't be," I coughed more blood, "if you are going to pray, pray that I make it a month. You take care now, Judd, live a long happy life for me, will you." He was a nice guy, I treated him the way I wanted to be treated, giving him a hug as I walked out the door.

"Farewell," he said.

"I'll see you in another life."

"I suppose you will."

Two weeks into the month of expectancy, my dog died, she too had cancer. Cleo was a beautiful dog, she kept the bed warm at night and my heart content the way no woman could. We spent days walking the driveway, down the road, and took trips to the park where she swam in the river. She was a good dog. We were both heavily doped up on narcotics for some time, I hoped selfishly that I would die first, that I did not have to bury her, but I did. An old willow tree out in the back forty she always ran to for some reason to spectate the land around, that was her final resting place.

She was a damn good dog.

Present day:

I thought I was truly alone until Cleo came into my life, Luis was still kicking strong, but I did not bother him with troubles. I wrote him a letter and had it placed on my typewriter after I finished the final page to my manuscript and shoved it in a manila folder. I would not have enough time to edit it, this was the end. Yesterday I took the coupe out for the last time and visited Maybelline's grave, placed flowers in a metal can and said goodbye for the last time in this life. My will had it so that

Luis got the coupe and any possessions he desired, I left him a final instruction as well, to deliver a copy of my final book to each of my sons. Walt would soon find out who his real father was and what had happened, James and Johnny too would know my story, hopefully find it in their hearts to forgive their old man. I left the house and property to the Oregon Humane Society, as long as they made it the largest operation in Oregon for dogs and cats to live and be adopted. The state agreed, when I die this land would become home to thousands of dogs and cats, my legacy. As far as the money and rights to my published works, I had that divided between my three sons and a sum of thirty thousand for each of my granddaughters.

Morphine only did so much for the pain, blood came up as I stood to my feet and walked over to the window where a branch still pestered, scratching and scratching. I saw my land, the sun was a white light where, in my doped-up lunacy, I saw Maybelline stick a hand out and say, "Hank, Hank, it's alright come along." She was still beautiful as ever, I could see that she forgave me for the horrible thing that I did, I forgave her too, sometimes two wrongs make a right. Hopefully, wherever I was destined to go, I would not have to remain a celibate; May and I could rekindle our fire, start anew. Blood saturated my lungs and flooded up the back of my throat, legs began to tremble, eyes felt like they were going to burst, I had my hands holding onto the curtain as I started to slip away, I could hardly breathe. I held on for dear life as I grabbed my last cigarette from behind my ear and lit it, blood stained the filter like cherry lipstick, I gagged as I inhaled a friendly accustomed flavor of tobacco. I stood there in the light of better days, my past behind me. This was the end of a long journey. Looping the curtain around an arm I propped against the wall, smoking my last smoke, this was the end—I sure as hell was not going to die on my knees and miss the sunset.

Epilogue:

Luis-

Hank was a hell of a character, we spent more nights drinking and smoking than I can recollect, he came into my life at a strange time, when I was simply a deputy under a dickhead chief. Hank and I grew to be brothers, I knew his wife well, before he shot her. He spent many nights contemplating suicide in prison, I gave him something to live for, in a sense, I told him he had to write, don't take away from society, give back. He had: his final novel "Diary Of A Dead Man" was his bestseller, it hit the charts with a fury. I knew the self-centered bastard would leave this world without a formal goodbye, I would've done the same.

Hank left me a letter with instructions: I gave each of his children a copy of his final book and the pseudonym so they could discover who their father was through his literature. Hank never had it easy, he got dealt the wrong hand after his brother died in that car wreck on his birthday. We never celebrated a birthday, Hank would only mourn and tell stories, drink himself into a three-day coma, mix in narcotics and tell me to keep a lid on it. I did, for him. If you have a best friend, you don't snitch on them, even if you are a small town cop.

Hank's kids come over to visit with me now, I tell them stories and explain who their father was. Hank would be relieved to know that with the power of his last book, his diary elaborated enough that his kids forgave him. All wished they would have known sooner, long before his death. Johnny was startled along with Walt to know he was the friendly old man that paid a visit every so often. Walt took it the hardest, having two dads die, but with time, he snapped out of his psychosis. James understood why his father did not interfere with the good life he had created, he only wished for a chance to say goodbye and apologize himself for not responding to the letters.

I buried my best friend next to his wife, watered the soil with whiskey and tears, and gave his casket a kiss goodbye. I named the boat I had been constructing for him as a birthday present, "Dead Man" after his pseudonym. It's too damn bad he kicked the bucket first. Hank always had to beat me, even in death. Life has grown rather quiet without Hank's rambunctious ass to get me drinking and driving, all the reckless activities that were inherent to his nature.

Hank was a hell of a man, and I will miss him.

Sincerely, Luis.

www.ingramcontent.com/pod-product-compliance
Lightning Source LLC
Chambersburg PA
CBHW032008240626
47153CB00003B/1175